Written by Sam Nisson

hmhbooks.com

Cover artwork by Chromosphere
Background design and layout by Elaine Lee
Character design by Keiko Murayama
Character color by Linda Fong
Additional help from Sylvia Liu and Eastwood Wong
Interior artwork by Artful Doodlers
Interior design by Chrissy Kurpeski
Art direction by Rachel Newborn

The text type was set in Adobe Garamond Pro.
The display type was set in Proxima Nova and CC Biff Bam Boom.

Library of Congress Cataloging-in-Publication data is on file.

ISBN: 978-1-328-62908-1 paper over board
ISBN: 978-1-328-62909-8 paperback

Printed in the United States of America
DOC 10 9 8 7 6 5 4 3 2 1
4500772049

CARMEN SANDIEGO™

CHASE YOUR OWN CAPER

HOUGHTON MIFFLIN HARCOURT

BOSTON NEW YORK

VILE PLOT

THE FIVE VILE INSTRUCTORS were gathered in the faculty lounge, discussing their latest defeat at the hands of Carmen Sandiego.

Coach Brunt, an enormously strong Texan who taught self-defense, shook her head sadly. "Black Sheep could have been VILE's best operative, then she had to go and betray her family. Sometimes I wonder where I went wrong."

"Let's not dwell in the past," snapped Professor Maelstrom, a gaunt man with a wicked face. "Black Sheep no longer exists. Now she is Carmen Sandiego, our sworn enemy, and she must be stopped *by any means necessary*."

"It will not be easy," grumbled Shadowsan, a grim Japanese man trained as a ninja. "Carmen Sandiego is fast, she is strong, and, most of all, she is smart."

"She also had the worst table manners of any student I can remember," said Countess Cleo, with her nose in the air. "To be honest, I never thought she'd amount to anything."

The fifth VILE instructor, Dr. Saira Bellum, wasn't paying attention to the conversation. She had five computer monitors open in front of her, tapping away at one with her left hand and another with her right hand, while looking at a third.

"Dr. Bellum," said Maelstrom wearily, "do *you* have anything to contribute?"

Bellum's specialty was science and gadgetry. "Oh, indeed I do," she said with a mad chuckle. "Perhaps our operatives will not be so worried about Carmen Sandiego—*once they are able to fly.*"

The four other instructors stared at Bellum blankly, waiting for her to explain.

"Jetpacks!" she exclaimed, waving her hands in the air. "Ten months ago, I hired a top technology company to build them according to my plans. The first jetpacks will be delivered tomorrow. Just imagine, VILE operatives will be able to strike from the sky at any time!"

"Well," said Countess Cleo with a sly smile, "I have always enjoyed looking down on people."

"Excellent," Maelstrom agreed. "It seems that we have some good news today after all."

Will VILE succeed in their plot to become flying criminals? In this story, it's up to you. Your choices will lead to one of twenty endings.

ARE YOU READY?

Turn to page **5**.

YOU ARE AN ENGINEER at Zeta Circuits, a technology company in Singapore.

You have lived your whole life in Singapore, a city at the southern tip of the Malay Peninsula in Asia. Long ago, the area belonged to fishermen and pirates, and later became part of a British colony. Today Singapore is its own country—your grandparents remember when it declared independence in 1965.

As one of the busiest ports in the world and a hub of high-tech manufacturing, Singapore is bursting with

opportunities for a smart engineer like you. In fact, you recently got the chance of a lifetime: a job on a top-secret project for Zeta Circuits.

You have been working on personal jetpacks, small enough to wear on your back, powerful enough to let a human fly like a bird. Although you are part of a large team, you have made important contributions, especially to the design of the rockets. After ten months of hard work, the jetpacks are finished.

Tonight you are working late, reviewing the results from the final flight tests—but after sixteen hours staring at numbers on your computer screen, you have dozed

off at your desk. You wake up disoriented, looking around your dimly lit office. All your coworkers are gone. Glancing at the clock on your computer, you see that it is 2:30 in the morning.

On the other side of the room, the door to the vault that holds the jetpacks is cracked open. *That's strange.* The vault has a thick metal door, which can only be unlocked by a fingerprint sensor. It's always supposed to be closed, to guard against high-tech spies and thieves. This doesn't make any sense, unless . . .

Unless there's a thief in the vault right now.

WHAT DO YOU DO?

▷ If you trigger an alarm,
   turn to page **20**.

▷ If you investigate yourself,
   turn to page **61**.

MAYBE CARMEN SANDIEGO is telling the truth, but you still can't let her walk out with the jetpack. You step back and grab the heavy metal door, swinging it shut to trap Carmen inside the vault.

With lightning speed, Carmen lifts her arm and a grappling hook shoots from her sleeve, lodging in the door frame so that the vault door can't close all the way. You are knocked backwards as she kicks the door open from the other side.

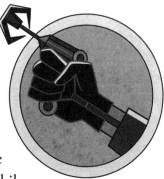

Carmen steps out of the vault carrying the jetpack while you stumble to your feet. "I know you're trying to do the right thing," she says. "But right now, stealing this jetpack is the right thing."

"Stealing is always wrong," you insist.

"Do me one favor," Carmen says. "Tomorrow, when you come into work, find out who you're building these for. After that, if you change your mind and decide to help me—"

"I'm not going to change my mind!"

"If you change your mind, call Sal's Pizza in Niagara Falls, Canada, and ask for the Buenos Aires Special. Good luck."

Before you can answer, Carmen dashes across the office floor and leaps through a circular hole that has been cut in the outside window. Running after her, you glimpse a shadowy figure gliding away over the rooftops. You are all alone in the dark office.

You call Zeta Circuits security, and within minutes the room is crowded with guards. You tell them that you noticed the vault door was open and that you saw someone escape through the window. You don't tell them, though, that you met Carmen Sandiego because you think she may have been telling the truth.

The next day, you ask to meet with your boss, an imposing woman who sits in a corner office with glass walls on two sides overlooking the city. "Well done reporting the theft last night," she says as you sit down. "You've done great work on the jetpack project, and I'm going to recommend you for a promotion."

"Thank you," you say. "That means a lot to me. I did have one question—"

"Yes?" she asks, already losing interest and looking back at her computer screen.

"Who are we building the jetpacks for?"

Your boss looks back at you with a cold stare. "Our client is an elite trading company that specializes in valuable imports and lavish exports."

"A trading company? Why do they need jetpacks?"

She wrinkles her nose as if smelling something foul. "That is none of your business. They hired us, they pay us, we deliver the jetpacks. End of story."

Your boss obviously doesn't want to talk about this, but you press on. "But what if they're criminals?" you ask. "The jetpacks are powerful. We should make sure that they're used in the right way."

Your boss leans back in her chair and folds her arms. "You know," she says, "on second thought, you're not a good fit here at Zeta Circuits. Your work is sloppy, and you have a bad attitude. In fact, you're fired. I want you out of here by noon."

As you walk back to your desk, you struggle not to cry in front of your coworkers. You gather your few things, take the elevator down, and walk out of the Zeta Circuits building for the last time. Your dream job is gone forever, all because you asked too many questions.

You decide that before looking for a new job, you will spend some time enjoying yourself and exploring your beautiful city. You spend lots of quality time with your cat, whom you named Mustard because her fur is white with orange splotches around the eyes and paws.

One sunny afternoon, you visit Singapore's famous Merlion statue, an imaginary creature with the head of a lion and the body and tail of a fish. The statue is twenty-eight feet tall, and a constant stream of water shoots out of its mouth into Marina Bay.

As you gaze up at the statue, you notice a man in a black suit and tie standing beneath a nearby tree. He's wearing dark sunglasses, but somehow you think that he's watching you. Are you being paranoid? You decide

to leave the area, but when you start walking, the man starts walking too. You cross a highway, heading deeper into the city. The man crosses right behind you.

Now in a fancy shopping neighborhood, you see another man coming toward you from the opposite direction, also dressed in a black suit and sunglasses. You turn onto an avenue, walking faster. Are they some sort of secret agents? Glancing over your shoulder, you see that a woman has joined the two men, and all three are walking quickly, matching your pace.

They're definitely following you. You dart into a cluster of tourists and dodge down a side street. Pressing yourself into a doorway to hide, you peek out to see the three agents talking and looking around. They don't know where you are, at least for the moment.

Maybe they're the police—or maybe they're VILE coming to get you for asking too many questions. You remember that Carmen invited you to call her if you ever decided to switch sides.

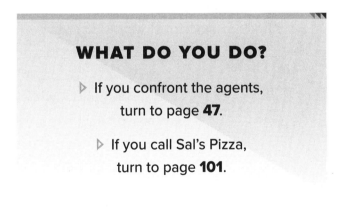

WHAT DO YOU DO?

▷ If you confront the agents,
turn to page **47**.

▷ If you call Sal's Pizza,
turn to page **101**.

*"**ABSOLUTELY NOT,**"* you say, your voice shaking with anger. "This night is out of control. We're going back to the plane. *Now!*"

Without looking back at Paperstar, you fly away from the broken skylight. You should have never stopped in Florence. How are you going to explain this to your boss at Zeta Circuits?

You're relieved when Paperstar flies up next to you. "I'm sorry I made stuff weird," she says, pulling another sheet of paper out of her pouch. She folds the paper into a complicated flower, which she holds out to you. "Please accept my apology."

"It's okay," you say. "Let's pretend this never happened."

As you reach for the flower, Paperstar yanks it away from you and jams it into the left engine of your jetpack. Immediately, you sputter and go into a violent spiral. You try to regain control, but with only one engine, it's impossible to stabilize and you start to tumble head over feet toward the Arno River below.

As you fall, you glimpse Paperstar hovering above you, smiling and waving goodbye.

THE END

"I CAN'T STOP THEM from taking off," you say. "I'm sorry."

"That's okay," Carmen reassures you. "We'll get them next time."

You watch the Zeta Circuits jet taxi out of the parking area toward a runway. Without knowing their next stop, there's no way you can follow.

"So, what now?" Zack asks glumly.

"Now VILE has jetpacks," says Carmen. "Once they learn how to use them, they'll try their first flying heist. We need to figure out some way to stop them."

"I've been wondering," Ivy says. "How do the jetpacks work? I mean, how do you control them when you're flying?"

"Each jetpack comes with a control glove," you explain, "that you wear on your right hand. Then you make different hand gestures to tell the jetpack what to do." You show them the gestures to start, stop, speed up, slow down, and turn. "Where's the jetpack that you stole in Singapore?" you ask Carmen. "I can teach you how to fly it."

"Unfortunately," says Zack, "this happened." He

opens an overhead storage bin and takes out the jetpack. It looks blobby and melted, with gobs of plastic blocking the jets. "Do you think it can still fly?"

"Oh no," you say, realizing what happened. "As a fail-safe, all the jetpacks have a self-destruct code that can be triggered remotely. Zeta Circuits must have destroyed this one as soon as it was stolen."

"Wait a minute!" says Ivy, jumping to her feet. "Maybe we could build something to trigger the self-destruct on the VILE jetpacks."

Everyone looks to you. You hadn't thought of that before, but it might be possible. "I don't think we could do it from across the world," you say. "But if we got close, we might be able to use a radio signal to override the controls and trigger the self-destruct. I know the encryption codes, so we would just need to build a transmitter."

Ivy smiles proudly. "I could build that in my sleep," she says.

"Let's get working," Carmen says. "We won't have much time before VILE is ready to make their first aerial strike."

Player finds you a workshop in an industrial area of

Nairobi, and you and Ivy start building. Ivy turns out to be a gifted tinkerer, and soon the device is done. It looks like a plastic box with an antenna and one big red button. Zack names it the *destructo-button*.

Hours later, Carmen gets an urgent message from Player. He has intercepted chatter on the Internet about VILE's first flying heist. As you gather around Carmen's laptop, Player explains that a shipyard in Brisbane, Australia, has just finished building a yacht called the *Golden Gull*. They say it's the most expensive ship ever build, with crystal chandeliers, Persian carpets, solid-gold door handles, and every other luxury you could imagine.

The *Golden Gull* is going to be delivered from Brisbane to a billionaire buyer in Fiji, a remote island nation in the South Pacific Ocean. VILE is planning to hijack it along the way. If you move quickly, you might be able to intercept VILE before they get to the yacht.

Twenty-four hours later, you, Carmen, Zack, and Ivy are on your own ship, called the *Narwhal*. You are on the Coral Sea, five hundred miles east of the Australian coast, sailing toward the area where VILE is supposed to ambush the *Golden Gull*.

You and Zack are on the *Narwhal*'s bridge watching your radar display, which sweeps the ocean to show any nearby ships. Carmen and Ivy are down on deck, scanning the ocean with high-powered binoculars. So far, you are the only ship within fifty miles.

A blip appears on your radar, another ship traveling in the same direction as you and gaining on you from behind. "Who is that?" Zack asks. "They're coming in really fast."

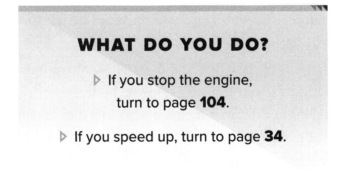

A voice crackles from your boat radio. "Unidentified ship," the voice says, "you are in the middle of a police action. Stop your engine *immediately* or you will be arrested!"

"What should we do?" Zack asks.

WHAT DO YOU DO?

▷ If you stop the engine, turn to page **104**.

▷ If you speed up, turn to page **34**.

YOU REACH UNDER your desk to press a hidden button. Immediately, bright lights flash and a Klaxon sounds—***ZEEP, ZEEP, ZEEP.***

Someone dashes out from the open vault. You glimpse a red coat and hat as the thief races across the room and leaps through a round hole that has been cut in the outside window of your twenty-ninth-floor office.

Twenty seconds later, the door to the hallway bursts open, and three security guards rush in. The lead guard shouts into her phone, "Code red on the twenty-ninth floor! Lock down all exits immediately!" She sees you standing dumbstruck in the middle of the room and barks, "You, *freeze!* Who are you?"

"I work here," you say shakily. "I'm the one who set off the alarm."

When it's clear that you don't know anything more about the theft, the guards send you home for the night. You walk in a daze through the dark streets of Singapore to your apartment. As you fall asleep with your cat, Mustard, curled up by your feet, you picture the mysterious thief streaking across your office and leaping fearlessly through the window.

When you get to work the next morning, you get a call that your boss wants to speak to you. She's an imposing woman who sits in a giant corner office, with two walls made entirely of glass looking out over the city.

She tells you what they know so far about the crime: the thief got in by cutting a hole in the outside window and then hacked the fingerprint scanner on the vault door. The good news, though, is that you scared the thief away when you triggered the alarm, so nothing was actually stolen.

"In other words," she says, smiling faintly, "you're a bit of a hero."

"Thank you," you say nervously, not mentioning that you were fast asleep at the time of the crime.

"I've been watching you," your boss says. "Your work is excellent. As you know, we are about to deliver three finished jetpacks to our client. I need one of my best engineers to oversee the delivery and answer any questions. I think you're the one for the job."

"Really, me?"

"You sound nervous. This is a big responsibility. Are you ready for it?"

"Yes!" you say. "One hundred percent. Where do I go?"

"The jetpacks are being delivered by private jet," she

says. "You take off from Changi Airport at ten o'clock." She checks her watch. "You better get moving."

At 9:50 you are in the cabin of a private jet, waiting on the runway. The inside of the jet is like a fancy hotel room, with big plush chairs, carpet on the floor, even a refrigerator for drinks and snacks. At the back of the cabin sits a black plastic crate with the three jetpacks inside, ready for delivery. You don't even know where you're going.

Your boss calls on your cellphone. "You're making a stop in Nairobi, Kenya, to pick up a passenger, someone who works for our client. Make sure to keep her happy, got it?"

"Got it," you say.

A few minutes later, the jet takes off and you are in the air. You open the crate with the jetpacks, making sure that everything is where it should be. Then you help yourself to a soda and an ice cream from the refrigerator and settle down into a big comfy chair.

The flight from Singapore to Nairobi takes more than nine hours, crossing the Indian Ocean between Asia and Africa. When you land, you wait in a parking area for your passenger to arrive. Finally, the jet's cabin door clicks open. You hop to your feet, ready to meet your guest.

A young woman steps into the cabin, dressed in a stylish, colorful outfit. "Welcome aboard," you say, holding out your hand to greet her. "On behalf of Zeta Circuits, I look forward to showing you our remarkable jetpacks. My name is—"

"I don't care," the young woman says, flopping herself into a chair. She pops a gum bubble as the cabin door pulls shut.

Remembering that you are supposed to keep your guest happy, you decide to try again. "So," you ask, "are you going to be part of the flight test? I think you'll be amazed when you get in the air for the first time."

She sighs loudly and puts in earbuds. The jet is moving again, picking up speed along the runway and then lifting into the air. The pilot speaks over the cabin loudspeaker. "We are approaching our cruising altitude of forty thousand feet. It looks like clear skies all the way to Reykjavik, Iceland."

"Wow," you say. "I've always wanted to visit Iceland!"

"A country named after ice," your guest replies sarcastically. "Sounds like a blast."

Now you're getting annoyed. "Actually," you say, "a lot of Iceland is green, but most of Greenland is covered in ice."

Your companion puts her face in her hands. "Please, tell me more incredible stories about countries and their names," she drones. "Like does everyone wear ties in Thailand?"

You decide not to talk to her anymore.

About an hour later, she picks up a newspaper and pulls off the top sheet. She folds it in half, then in half again, then starts folding in the corners. Soon her hands are moving so fast that you can't follow what she's doing, and a few seconds later, she has folded the paper into a perfect figure of a person—a person wearing a jetpack.

She tosses the figure across the cabin to you. It glides like a paper airplane and lands in your lap. "Listen," she says. "I have a great idea."

"Okay," you say skeptically.

"In Iceland, we're going to learn about the jetpacks and do a lot of boring flight tests, right? Fly up, fly down, fly here, fly there—so dull. I'd rather do a real test out in the field, if you know what I mean."

You have no idea what she means.

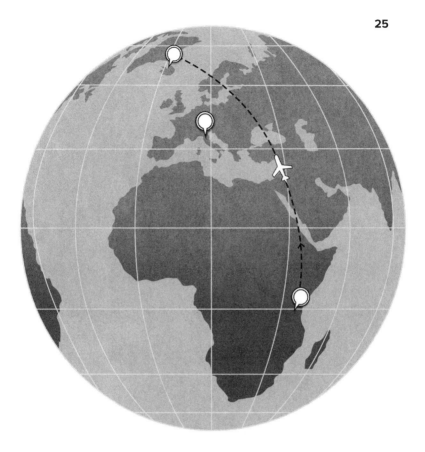

"I'm looking at our flight path," she says. "We're fly-ing right over Italy. Let's make a quick stop in Florence. That's where we should test the jetpacks. Wouldn't you rather fly over Florence's famous cathedral than a bunch of glaciers?"

"I can't do that," you say, although you would love to see Florence. "I'm not in charge of that stuff."

"Come on," she insists. "Just tell the pilot there's

been a change of plans and that we're making a quick stop. The pilot works for Zeta Circuits, right? He has to listen to you." As you consider, she adds, "By the way, my name is Paperstar."

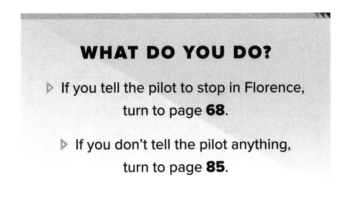

WHAT DO YOU DO?

▷ If you tell the pilot to stop in Florence, turn to page **68**.

▷ If you don't tell the pilot anything, turn to page **85**.

You wish you had trusted Carmen Sandiego last time, and you're not about to make the same mistake again. She smiles as you approach. "Hello," she says, holding out her hand. "I believe we met at your office in Singapore."

"Yes, we did," you say. "And you were right about everything. VILE is using the jetpacks to steal. In fact, they're coming here—"

Carmen interrupts you. "Let's not talk about business. This is a party."

Looking around, you notice a few people glancing at you curiously. You realize that you are talking too loudly and that you need to calm down. "Of course," you say. "Isn't this building amazing?"

"People always want to reach higher," Carmen says. "Did you know that when the Eiffel Tower was finished in 1889, it was the tallest structure in the world? It wasn't topped until 1929, when the Chrysler Building in New York went about sixty feet higher. Now we have this, the Burj Khalifa, almost as tall as three Eiffel Towers."

"Incredible," you agree. "I wonder what people will build next."

TALLEST OVER TIME

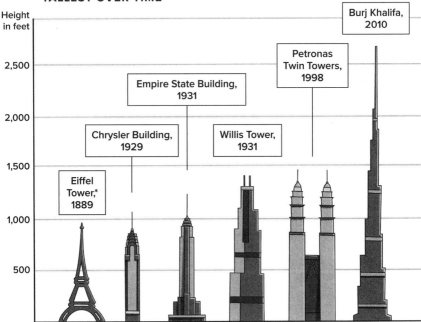

*The Chrysler Building was taller than the Eiffel Tower when it opened, but then in 1957, an antenna was added to the top of the Eiffel Tower, making it taller again.

Carmen gestures toward an open door. "Shall we step out on the balcony to enjoy the view?"

The wide balcony is surrounded by a glass wall, taller than a person. Through the glass you have a breathtaking view of the city of Dubai, a cluster of skyscrapers nearby, and then the water of the Persian Gulf beyond. There are fewer people on the balcony, and you find a quiet corner to talk. "I'm sorry about what happened in

Singapore," you tell Carmen. "I should have listened to you."

"All that matters now is what happens here," Carmen says. "The jewels are right there." She points out ten marble pedestals, each with a silver case on top. The pedestals are lined up against the glass wall of the balcony, blocked off from the party by a velvet rope, with an imposing guard on either side.

"They think the jewels are safe up here," you say, "a thousand feet in the sky. For flying thieves, though, they're an easy target."

"Exactly. We're on the 112th floor," she says, looking up. "But this building has more than 160 floors. I'm going higher. Maybe I can get the drop on them from above."

"What should I do?" you ask.

"Keep your eyes open," Carmen replies. "When the time comes, trust your instincts."

After Carmen disappears into the crowd, Agent Zari taps you on the shoulder. "Who were you talking to?" she asks.

"Someone I met at the party," you say. "I'm trying to blend in."

"Is that right?" Zari asks suspiciously. "Well, that *someone* happens to be Carmen Sandiego, maybe the greatest thief in the entire world. If she's here, she's leading the whole operation."

"That's not true," you say.

"Where did she go?" Zari asks, looking around with alarm. "She was right here a second ago, and now she's gone! Did she say anything to you? Did she tell you where she was going?"

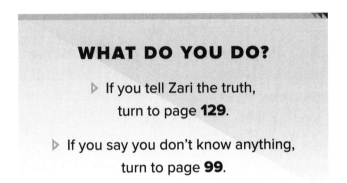

WHAT DO YOU DO?

▷ If you tell Zari the truth,
turn to page **129**.

▷ If you say you don't know anything,
turn to page **99**.

YOU SPIKE THE METAL BALL overhand into the watering hole, where it lodges in the mud, crackling with electricity. Suddenly, bolts of electric energy shoot out from the ball and into the water with a loud **ZAP.**

"What was *that?*" Zack gasps.

"It's called a crackle ball," Carmen explains. "One of Dr. Bellum's toys. It was supposed to shock all of us. Smart move throwing it into the watering hole—all of the electricity was conducted into the water."

The VILE guard charges at Carmen. She sidesteps him easily, tripping him into the dirt. Mime Bomb puts his fists up, like a boxer getting ready to fight.

"Come on, Mime Bomb," says Carmen cheerfully. "We both know Self-Defense wasn't your best class."

Mime Bomb frowns pitifully and mimes wiping his eyes like he's crying. Then he throws his hands up in the air in surrender. Ivy takes the crate with the jetpacks and loads it into the back of your SUV, and a few minutes later, you are on the highway back to Nairobi.

"That was awesome, you guys," Ivy cheers.

"Another win for Team Carmen," says Zack. "Safari time! I am not leaving Kenya until I see a hippopotamus."

"Maybe we can safari from the sky!" Ivy says. "Don't forget, we're carrying a crate of jetpacks in the back. Speaking of which—are the jetpacks making a weird sound?"

Zack pulls over the SUV. Without the hum of the engine, you clearly hear a hissing noise from inside the crate with the jetpacks. Carmen pulls the crate out of the back and flips it open. Inside, the jetpacks look like they're melting, with black plastic dripping in globs out of the rockets.

"It's the self-destruct," you say with alarm. "In case the jetpacks fell into the wrong hands, we built in a trigger to destroy them remotely."

"I guess we're the wrong hands," Carmen says. "The same thing happened to the one that I stole in Singapore."

"So that's it," says Ivy. "Nobody gets a jetpack. They're all destroyed."

"Well, there is one more," you say. "It's a prototype—the first one that we ever built. We keep it in a separate high-security building."

"Could Zeta Circuits use the prototype as a model to build more jetpacks for VILE?" Carmen asks.

"Oh definitely," you reply. "It has all the major systems—the air compressors, the control glove, the stabilizers."

Carmen thinks it over. "In that case, we need to steal that prototype jetpack, too. Looks like we're off on another caper."

"Hold on," Ivy says to you. "You still work at Zeta Circuits, right? Maybe you could snatch the prototype somehow."

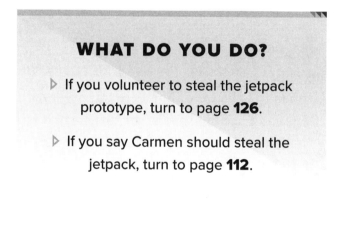

WHAT DO YOU DO?

▷ If you volunteer to steal the jetpack prototype, turn to page **126**.

▷ If you say Carmen should steal the jetpack, turn to page **112**.

"KEEP GOING," you tell Zack. "Actually, go faster."

Zack pushes the throttle forward, the engines rumbling as the *Narwhal* speeds up. Carmen races into the bridge. "What's happening?" she asks.

"Someone's following us," Zack says. "And it looks like they're faster." Sure enough, the blip on the radar is getting closer again.

Carmen calls Player on speakerphone. "Player?" she asks. "Are you tracking that ship on our radar?"

"Sure am," Player says. *"They'll be in visual range in just a few minutes."*

"Can you scramble their navigation?"

"I don't know. I'm locked on to their system, but they've got a double firewall with level-five encryption . . . hang on . . . hang on . . . okay, done! Their radar and navigation are down. It should be at least thirty minutes for them to reboot their systems. Until then, they're sailing blind."

"Amazing," Carmen cheers. "Next stop, VILE."

Twenty minutes later, Ivy calls from the deck that she has spotted the VILE ship. If you both keep going in the same direction, your paths will cross. Carmen peers at them with high-powered binoculars as you get closer.

"I spy a bunch of old friends," she says. "Looks like Le Chèvre . . . Paperstar . . . Neal the Eel." She hands you the binoculars. Sure enough, there are three people out on deck. One of them, a tall man with a beard, flies twenty feet into the air and then lands nimbly, practicing with his jetpack.

You spot a fourth person through the window of the ship's cabin. She's a small woman with a shock of white hair, wearing a lab coat and round glasses. "There's

someone else," you say, passing the binoculars back to Carmen. "Look inside the cabin."

Carmen refocuses the binoculars and then gasps in surprise. "What?" you ask. "Who is it?"

"That's Dr. Saira Bellum," Carmen says with amazement. "She's one of VILE's leaders. She almost never leaves their headquarters, so she must have really wanted to see this for herself."

The two ships are now only a few hundred feet apart. The VILE ship blows a loud horn, telling you to get out of the way. "Okay," Carmen says. "Our only chance is to use the destructo-button at the right time to melt their jetpacks. I'm going to get them in the air. Ivy, you be ready with that button."

Ivy holds up her pointer finger. "Ready to press!" she says.

Carmen stands, so that she is in plain view. She waves cheerfully to the three VILE operatives. "Excuse me," she shouts over the waves. "We're a little lost. Do any of you know the way to Bora-Bora?"

"Black Sheep!" says Le Chèvre. "We keep running into each other in the most unlikely places."

"You can't catch me on land," Carmen quips. "So, I thought I'd give you a chance at sea."

"Or perhaps," Le Chèvre gloats, "we shall catch you in the sky." He raises a hand and streaks up into the air. Paperstar and Neal the Eel follow. The three VILE operatives fly toward you, circling your ship like birds of prey, and then hover next to the *Narwhal*, twenty feet above the water.

"As you can see," Le Chèvre says, chuckling, "we've learned some new tricks since you left VILE Academy."

"Ivy, now," Carmen says calmly. Ivy presses the destructo-button.

Nothing happens. Ivy presses the button again. "What's going on?" Zack asks. "Shouldn't they be self-destructing about now?"

Paperstar laughs. "Silly Carmen," she says. "Dr. Bellum discovered the self-destruct trigger on the first day and took it out. Aw, did you really think you were going to blow us up? So sad."

Carmen sprints toward the edge of the *Narwhal*. She leaps up onto the railing and pushes off with one leg, hurtling through the air toward Paperstar. The VILE operative flies up, but not quite in time, and Carmen catches onto her legs.

Paperstar shrieks and kicks as Carmen dangles beneath her, the jetpack laboring to keep them both in the air. "Get her off me!" Paperstar shouts. Carmen swings herself up, wrapping her legs around Paperstar like a wrestler, and the two of them spin in the air. Finally, Carmen is thrown off, landing hard on the deck of the *Narwhal*.

"You're going to pay for that," Paperstar snarls, hovering in the air above Carmen.

Carmen holds up her hand and smiles. She's wearing Paperstar's control glove. She must have pulled it off while they were wrestling. Now Carmen can control Paperstar's jetpack. When Paperstar realizes what happened, her eyes widen with fear.

Using the hand gestures that you taught her, Carmen turns Paperstar upside down and then shakes her like a saltshaker. *"Help meeeeeeee . . ."* Paperstar hollers. Le Chèvre and Neal the Eel circle closer, looking for an opening to strike at Carmen.

"Smash them into each other," you shout. Carmen nods and sends Paperstar hurtling through the air directly at Le Chèvre. Rather than collide with her fellow operative, Paperstar takes off her jetpack, splashing into the water while the jetpack clatters onto the deck of the *Narwhal*, right at your feet.

WHAT DO YOU DO?

▷ If you put on the jetpack,
turn to page **134**.

▷ If you give the jetpack to Carmen,
turn to page **63**.

ACTIVATING THE TURBO BOOST is too risky a mile high in the sky, so you follow the VILE operative as closely as you can. He glides diagonally downward, toward a sparkling line of hotels that have been built on artificial islands at the edge of the city. Among those glittering lights, it's even harder to keep track of your target.

For a moment, you lose him, and then you see his flickering figure dive toward a fancy hotel courtyard. *Maybe that's where he's taking the jewels.* You cruise above the hotel, watching the VILE operative as he spirals gently down toward the pool.

This might be your best chance. Tucking into a power dive, you use your jetpack engines to blast directly downward. The operative sees you and tries to dodge. You wrap your arms around him — but he's wearing a black bodysuit that is ridiculously slippery, like it's covered in grease. He squirts out of your grasp and flies up again.

Off balance, you tumble into a midair back flip, spinning round and round like a pinwheel. By the time you steady yourself, the VILE operative is gone, impossible to spot against the black of the night sky.

You hear clapping from below. All around the edges of the pool, hotel guests are watching you. A little boy holding his father's hand is jumping up and down and pointing. "Do it again!" the boy shouts.

Why not? You fly up about a hundred feet, and this time go into an intentional forward somersault, flipping round and round as you fall toward the pool, and then pulling yourself up a moment before you hit the water. The hotel guests applaud wildly, more people coming out into the courtyard to see what the fuss is about.

For fifteen minutes, you put on a show. You buzz the hotel balconies at top speed. You pick up a beach ball, drop it from three hundred feet, and then zoom down to catch it yourself. You lift the little boy and give him a gentle ride around the pool before dropping him into his father's arms. "More!" he shouts.

When you run out of ideas, a woman in a suit waves for your attention. She introduces herself as the hotel manager and says that she is always looking for new entertainment. She asks if you'd be interested in putting on a daily show at the hotel—offering to pay you more than your old job.

You say that you'll do it. You lost your old job anyway, so why not try something new? Plus, a daily flying show sounds like a lot more fun.

THE END

"I DON'T KNOW ANYTHING about any super criminals," you say. "Now, if you don't mind, I'd like to get back to the *Narwhal*. I was right in the middle of a game of solitaire."

Zari looks annoyed. "When our operation is complete, we'll return you to your ship. In the meantime, you're coming with us."

"Should we search the *Narwhal*?" another agent asks.

"There's no time," says Zari. "We need to catch up with VILE before they get to the *Golden Gull*. Full speed ahead!"

The *Gumshoe*'s engines spit foam as you jump forward, gliding through the choppy water. You watch as your ship, with your friends onboard, gets smaller behind you, and then disappears in the distance.

"Ship ho!" shouts one of the agents. Sure enough, you see a speck across the water, ahead and to the right.

"That should be VILE," Zari barks. "Set a course to intercept, full speed."

As you get closer, an agent reports to Zari, "They're not even trying to run. At this rate, we'll be on them in minutes."

You are so close now to the VILE ship that you can see three people on deck. One of them waves to you. "Okay, everyone," Zari says, "this is our big chance! Let's make Chief proud. Launch the EMP torpedo!"

"You have an EMP torpedo?" you ask an agent standing nearby.

"Correct," the agent replies. "It uses an electromagnetic pulse to knock out all of a ship's electrical systems and stop it dead in the water." A moment later, you hear a *whoosh* and see a dark shape zoom under the surface of the water toward the VILE ship. There's a flash of light beneath the hull, and then the ship stops moving.

"Direct hit!" Zari shouts as all the agents cheer. "Let's bring them in!"

The three people on the VILE ship run inside the cabin in alarm. A few moments later, they lift into the air, two of them carrying a fourth person between them. They soar high over the ocean, flying away from the *Gumshoe*. "What is *that?*" Zari shouts. "What am I seeing?"

"They're people," says an agent who is looking through binoculars. "Um, flying people."

"Follow them!" Zari hollers. "Don't let them get away!"

The *Gumshoe* turns to chase, but the jetpacks are faster than the ship, and the VILE operatives soon disappear in the distance. Thirty minutes later, a breathless agent dashes out from the *Gumshoe*'s cabin. "We have a distress call from the captain of the *Golden Gull*," the agent tells Zari. "He says that he's been boarded by . . . by pirates from the sky."

Zari drops her face into her hands and shakes her head in frustration. "Chief is not going to be happy about this," she moans.

With VILE long gone, you take the long voyage back to Australia on the *Gumshoe*. An agent drops you at the airport with a stern warning not to tell anyone about anything that you have seen.

Days later, you are back in your own cozy apartment, in your home city of Singapore. You are working on your laptop, looking for a new job. Your cat, Mustard, presses her head against your leg and meows, begging for attention. "Give me a minute," you tell her.

An email pops up in your inbox.

Thanks for covering for us on our ocean adventure. VILE got away this time, but you gave us a chance to fight another day.

I'm sorry that I put you in danger. Good luck finding a new job. I know you'll do great things — hopefully not building any more secret tech for evil criminals.

Your friend,

Carmen Sandiego

You smile and tab back to the job listings.

THE END

THIS IS RIDICULOUS. You haven't done anything wrong, and you're not going to be chased around
the streets of your own city. You leave your hiding spot
and stride up to the three agents, who turn toward you
with blank expressions. "Who are you?" you demand.
"And why are you following me?"

"You need to come with us," the woman says. She
glances down subtly at a device that she is holding in her
hand, some sort of electric stun gun. The two men move
to either side of you, each taking one of your arms.

The three agents guide you on a winding path
through the city, until you arrive at stairs that lead
down to a basement door. The woman gestures for you
to go in.

"What's down there?" you ask.

"Down the stairs, through the door," she replies.
"Everything will be explained."

You walk down the stairs. One of the agents knocks,
and the door swings open. Inside, you see a square room
with concrete walls, floor, and ceiling, a metal chair, and
a single lightbulb dangling overhead.

"Sit down," orders one of the agents. You've come
this far. What choice do you have?

After you sit, the woman pulls a pen out of her pocket, which she clicks and drops onto the floor. A cone of bright blue light shines upward from the pen and then condenses into the shape of a person—a woman in a business suit with a stern face. The hologram woman considers you for a few seconds with an iron stare.

"You're the engineer from Zeta Circuits?" she asks.

"I used to be," you say. "Who in the world are you?"

"Call me Chief," she says in a commanding voice. "I understand that you worked on Zeta's top-secret jetpack project."

"How do you know about that?" you gasp.

"It's my job to know things," she says. "Did you know that Zeta Circuits sold those jetpacks to an organization called VILE, ultra-powerful criminals who are now using your technology to commit aerial crimes around the world?"

"Hold on," you say, standing up. "Am I in trouble? I swear I didn't know who the jetpacks were for."

"Sit down!" Chief barks. "I called you here because we are trying to stop VILE and we need your help. A few days ago, this yacht was captured at sea." She gestures, and an image appears in the air, a ship with a golden hull sailing on the ocean.

"The *Golden Gull*," Chief explains. "Supposedly the

most expensive ship ever built. The captain was left floating on a lifeboat in the middle of the ocean. He says that the thieves *flew* over the water and landed on his ship."

You gasp. "They must have used the jetpacks!"

"Precisely," Chief says. "And if I know VILE, they are just getting started. Except that we are going to stop them. Right?"

"Right," you say. "What can I do?"

"We know that VILE's next target is an exclusive jewel auction at the Burj Khalifa, the tallest building in

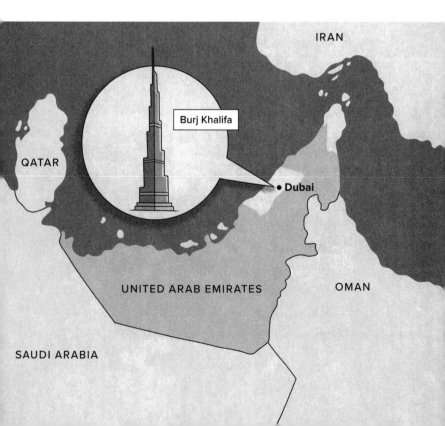

the world. I am sending a team to Dubai to catch VILE. I want you to go with them."

"I'm just an engineer," you say. "Why me?"

"You know better than anyone how the jetpacks work," Chief explains. "You may be able to spot a weakness in VILE's attack."

Fifteen hours later, you step from the elevator into a party on the 112th floor of the Burj Khalifa, in Dubai. You are a guest at the jewel auction, wearing clothing that costs more than your monthly salary. You gaze at the other guests, men and women in tuxedos and evening gowns and sparkling jewelry. You recognize a famous actress from an American television show. How are you supposed to blend in here?

One of the ACME agents who captured you in Singapore is here too, standing by the food table, looking uncomfortable in a black dress. Her name is Agent Zari, but you're supposed to pretend that you don't know each other.

A young woman in a beautiful red evening gown catches your eye, her hair up in an elaborate knot, a string of garnets around her neck. She looks familiar, but you can't place her. Another famous actress, maybe?

And then you remember—it's the thief from the vault in Singapore. It's Carmen Sandiego.

WHAT DO YOU DO?

▷ If you talk to Carmen,
turn to page **27**.

▷ If you avoid her,
turn to page **94**.

YOU STEP ASIDE to let Carmen leave the vault.

"Thank you," she says. "I promise, you're doing the right thing." Carrying the jetpack, she walks across the office to a round hole that has been cut in the outside window.

"Wait!" you say. "That's not the only jetpack. There are three more, but they're already on their way to our client—to VILE."

Carmen turns, looking worried. "Where are they being sent?" she asks.

"I don't know," you tell her. "I really don't. I heard that they were being loaded onto a private jet, but I have no idea where they're going."

"Okay," says Carmen. "Thank you. I'll take care of it."

Moving quickly, she dives through the hole in the window. You race after her to see where she's going, but glimpse only a shadow gliding away into the night.

The next day, before work, you take an early morning walk through East Coast Park, one of your favorite places in Singapore. The park runs along the water of the busy Singapore Strait. You like watching the dozens of cargo ships pass by, imagining what each one is carrying and where it's going.

You dread going back to work. How will you explain that you saw the thief but didn't try to stop her? You're going to have to lie to everyone. Maybe you'll say that you slept through the whole thing, which is embarrassing but better than admitting that you helped a criminal. Maybe you'll call in sick.

Your phone buzzes. The call is coming from Niagara Falls, Canada, and the name on the screen reads "Sal's Pizza."

"Hello," you answer.

"Hi there," says a friendly voice, which sounds like a teenage boy. *"Is this the jetpack engineer who works at Zeta Circuits?"*

"Who wants to know?" you ask suspiciously.

"You can call me Player. I'm a friend of Carmen Sandiego. You met her last night. She's a super thief—wears a lot of red?"

"I remember her," you say.

"Oh great," Player says. *"Anyway, I've been poking around in some of your company's computer systems— "*

"How did you get into our computer systems?" you interrupt. "How old are you?"

"We can talk about your security holes some other time. The point is, a Zeta Circuits jet took off

from Changi Airport in Singapore just a few minutes ago. We think it's probably carrying the rest of the jetpacks."

"Okay," you say. "What does that have to do with me?"

"According to the flight plan, the jet is headed for Nairobi, Kenya. Carmen wants to snatch the jetpacks before they're handed off to VILE. She wants you to go with her. She says that it would be good to have an expert along on the mission, and that you have a heroic quality. Those were her exact words, heroic quality.*"*

You've never thought of yourself as a hero. "I don't know," you say. "I already helped Carmen once, and it might cost me my job."

"Maybe this will be better than your job," Player suggests. *"Anyway, Carmen is flying out from Changi Airport in half an hour. We hope you'll be there!"*

WHAT DO YOU DO?

▷ If you meet Carmen at the airport, turn to page **119**.

▷ If you go to work, turn to page **83**.

"I'LL DO IT," you say. "But we need to get out of here, fast."

"Don't worry about that," Bellum says. "I assure you that my ship can outrun that rented tub your friends are in." She pushes her ship's throttle to full speed, and you feel the engines roar beneath your feet. Looking across the water, you see Carmen, Zack, and Ivy on the deck of the *Narwhal,* jumping and waving. They must be totally confused.

"What about your operatives?" you ask. "The ones in the water."

"I'm sure Carmen Sandiego will pull them out," Bellum says. "She was always soft that way."

The *Narwhal* follows you, but as Bellum promised, her ship is faster. Soon, your former friends are lost in the distance. "Where are we going?" you ask.

"Iceland," she tells you. "You're going to need some warmer clothes."

The boat docks in Fiji, where you take a plane to Reykjavik, and then a helicopter to a remote fjord in northwestern Iceland. You find yourself on a high cliff overlooking the ocean, with one tiny building made of metal.

"Welcome to your new home," Bellum says. "Don't worry about the size. Most of the action is underground."

Inside the metal building, you find a single room containing a table and chairs, a refrigerator—and an elevator. Bellum presses the call button. When the elevator arrives, there are only two buttons inside, marked *S* and *U*. "For *surface* and *underground*," she explains.

She presses U. The elevator moves for a few seconds and then opens onto an enormous underground chamber carved from rock. In the center of the room stands a giant robot, fifty feet tall and made of gleaming metal. People in lab coats scurry back and forth around the room, carrying parts and looking at tablet computers.

"We haven't been able to get the robot to walk on its own yet," Bellum explains. "Balance is difficult. But we make progress every day."

You walk to the robot's feet and stare up at its massive height. An engineer sits on its shoulder, welding something onto its head with a shower of sparks. "I am putting you in charge of the laser cannons," Bellum says. "I want them to shoot out of the robot's eyes. Do you think you can handle that?"

"Yes," you say. "I think I can."

YOUR ALARM GOES OFF at 6:30—time to wake up.

Last night, there was a robbery at Zeta Circuits, where you work. At least you think it was last night. Somehow you feel like it was a longer time ago. But you don't remember anything happening since, so it must have been last night.

As you pour yourself a bowl of cereal, you wonder again who the thief was, and whether they were caught. You're glad they didn't get away with the jetpacks, which are ready to be delivered after so much work.

Your cat rubs against your leg and meows. She's mostly white, with orange splotches on her paws and around her eyes. She jumps on the table and sniffs your cereal. You got her from an animal shelter when she was just a kitten.

"Hey, there," you say, scratching the back of her head. "I know you're hungry, but you won't like my cereal."

She meows as you get a can of food from the cabinet and open it, filling her bowl. "Okay, here you go . . . Here you go . . ."

What is your cat's name? Strangely, you can't remember, even though you are 100 percent sure she's your cat. You have a feeling that it starts with an *M. Muffin, Mittens, Molly.* None of those sounds right.

You'll have to think about it more later. You pull on your shoes and head out for work.

YOU CREEP ACROSS THE OFFICE, past the rows of computers. The door to the vault is open only a crack, a strip of light shining from inside.

Peeking inside, you gasp with surprise. A young woman is in the vault, wearing a red hat and a red coat. Usually there are four jetpacks in the vault, but today there is only one because the other three are on their way to be delivered. The jetpack hangs on a mannequin, locked to the wall by a thin metal cord. The woman in red has her back to you as she works intensely on the lock.

"It's rude to stare," she says. "You should introduce yourself."

There's a metallic click as the lock pops open. The woman takes the jetpack off the mannequin and turns to face you. "I'll go first," she says. "My name is Carmen Sandiego."

"Thief!" you say. "You can't take that."

"Do you know who this jetpack is for?" Carmen asks you.

Oddly, you don't know. Your boss

has told you that the jetpacks are being sold to a wealthy, secretive client, but she hasn't told you the name of the client or what they plan to do with the jetpacks.

"The jetpacks are for VILE," Carmen tells you. "They're a criminal organization—rich, ruthless, and very dangerous. If they learn how to fly, they'll become unstoppable. I'm making sure that never happens."

Something in Carmen's face makes you want to believe her—but how can you trust this thief who showed up in the middle of the night?

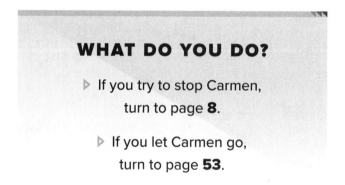

WHAT DO YOU DO?

▷ If you try to stop Carmen,
turn to page **8**.

▷ If you let Carmen go,
turn to page **53**.

YOU SLIDE THE JETPACK across the deck to Carmen. She straps it on her back and makes a gesture with the control glove to take off into the sky. Although you showed her the control gestures, Carmen has never used a jetpack before, and she is clearly unsteady in the air.

Le Chèvre circles around her. "No one challenges Le Chèvre in the sky," he says. "Prepare for the battering ram." Lowering his head, he blasts toward Carmen at full speed. Carmen bobs out of the way, then spins like a top and kicks Le Chèvre in the back as he passes. She keeps spinning, round and round, and when she finally stops, she looks dizzy.

Meanwhile, Neal the Eel is creeping toward Carmen from below, looking for a chance to strike. Carmen dives to tackle him, wrapping her arms around his waist. Somehow, though, he pops out of her grip, as though he's too slippery to hold. Carmen wobbles above the surface of the water as she tries to regain her balance.

Le Chèvre speeds toward her again, this time from above. He grabs her by both shoulders and dunks her into the water. You hear a crackle as Carmen's jetpack engines short out, leaving her bobbing helplessly in the waves.

Ivy throws Carmen a life preserver. Meanwhile, Paperstar has climbed back onto the VILE ship. Le Chèvre hovers over your heads, smiling. "I always said Black Sheep was overrated," he gloats. "Now we must go. We have a ship to steal."

The VILE operatives streak away through the sky while Carmen, soaking wet, pulls herself back up onto the deck of the *Narwhal*. You know that VILE is going to get away with stealing the *Golden Gull*, and you wish that, somehow, you could have done more to stop them.

THE END

YOU'LL ONLY GET one chance at this. You point yourself as best you can toward the VILE operative and trigger the turbo boost. Your jetpack roars as you shoot forward at double speed, totally out of control. You ram into the VILE operative from behind with a metallic crunch.

The two of you bounce apart. The VILE operative's jetpack starts to sputter—damaged in the collision—and he wobbles in the air. You zoom forward to catch him, but he's wearing a black bodysuit that's impossibly slippery, and you can't get a grip. "Take my hand," you say.

He grabs your hand, just as his jetpack groans and dies. Dangling beneath you, the man says, "My name is Neal the Eel. Please, don't drop me."

"I won't," you say. "I promise."

Holding Neal's hand tightly, you fly toward the Burj Khalifa. When you get back to the balcony with the party, the smoke has cleared, and the guests are gone. Agent Zari walks around giving orders. You drop Neal the Eel onto the balcony, where he is surrounded by ACME agents.

"I'm impressed," Zari says.

"What happened to the other VILE operatives?" you ask.

"We caught two of them," she says. "Unfortunately, Carmen Sandiego got away. We also lost a million-dollar diamond necklace that flew off the balcony during the fight. Still, I'd say it was a win overall."

You wait as the agents snap pictures of the crime scene and take Neal the Eel away. Fifteen minutes later, Zari hands you a pen. "Someone wants to talk to you," she says. You click the pen and drop it, like you saw Zari do earlier. A holographic Chief appears next to you on the balcony.

"Well, well," says Chief. "I hear that you made a mile-high arrest. Sounds like you're a lot more than just an engineer."

"I'm happy I could help," you say.

"I'm starting a special flying unit within ACME," Chief says. "We're going to build jetpacks of our own and train an elite squad of flying agents. I'd like you to join us permanently to lead the squad. Will you do it?"

"I'll do it," you say.

"Excellent," says Chief. "From now on, when we fight VILE, we'll always have the high ground."

THE END

YOU OPEN THE DOOR that connects the cabin to the cockpit. The pilot, surprised to see you, looks up from his controls. "What can I do for you?" he asks.

"There's been a change of plans," you say. "We need to make a quick stop in Florence."

The pilot looks skeptical. "Florence? They just told me to go to Iceland!"

"The order came from my boss at Zeta Circuits," you insist. "She said that it's extremely important."

"Roger that," he says with a shrug. "I'll call ahead to clear us for landing."

You turn back to the cabin. "Guess what?" you tell Paperstar. "We're going to Italy!"

She claps her hands merrily. "I liked you from the beginning," she says. "We are going to have so much fun."

It's dark when you land at the airport in Florence. You take two jetpacks from their storage crate and step outside the jet onto a concrete parking area. You've been traveling for over twenty hours and are grateful to stretch your legs and breathe the outdoor air.

Paperstar takes one of the jetpacks and straps it on. It looks like a black backpack made of plastic. "How does it work?" she asks, frowning. You look around to make sure no one's watching. The runway is deserted.

"I'll show you," you say, strapping the second jetpack onto your back. "First, you need the control glove. It's in a compartment on the side of your jet-pack—right here." Each of you finds your control glove and pulls it on.

"The control glove talks to the jetpack," you explain. "Different hand gestures tell it to start, stop, turn. For instance—"

You clap your hands and then give a thumbs-up with your right hand. The thrusters on your jetpack come to life, shoot-ing you into the air and then slowing down at your command, so that you are hovering ten feet above the ground.

"Sweet!" exclaims Paperstar. Imitating your hand gestures, she joins you up in the air. "Teach me every-thing."

You teach Paperstar the gestures to take off and land, and how to steer while in the air. She learns quickly and within an hour is flying expertly. "We're in Italy," she says as she makes lazy circles over your head. "Let's go see the sights."

As the two of you soar above the airport, the historic city of Florence comes into view. You know that some of humankind's greatest artists lived and worked here, artists like Michelangelo and Leonardo da Vinci. Almost every rooftop is covered with the same reddish clay tiles, giving the whole city a warm, welcoming glow.

In the distance, you spot the brightly lit dome of the Duomo, Florence's famous cathedral, rising above the surrounding buildings. "This way," Paperstar calls as she zooms toward the Arno, a river that flows through the city. You follow, feeling giddy as the cool night air brushes past your face. Down below, lights glimmer off the surface of the water. You can see people crossing bridges and gathering in squares.

You pass above the Ponte Vecchio, a covered bridge across the Arno River that was built in medieval times. "There's the Uffizi," you shout to Paperstar, pointing to a horseshoe-shaped building on the edge of the river. "Some of art's greatest treasures are in there, like Botticelli's painting of the goddess Venus."

"Sounds fab," Paperstar quips. "Let's have a look."

"I'm sure it's closed this time of night—"

Paperstar isn't listening. She tucks into a dive and zips toward the Uffizi's roof. She really did master her jetpack quickly. You follow her down to where she is hovering, twenty feet over a skylight.

"Do you know why rock, scissors, paper is a dumb game?" she asks. When you don't answer, she tells you with a wicked smile, "Because paper beats everything." She pulls a sheet of paper from a pouch she wears on her belt. Fingers moving in a blur, she folds it into a throwing star, which she whips at the glass of the skylight.

ZIP, ZIP, ZIP—ten more throwing stars follow, and then a cut piece of the skylight falls away with a crash onto the Uffizi floor. "Let's go see some art," she says, drifting down toward the hole.

"What in the world are you doing?" you holler. "You're breaking into the Uffizi! That's a *crime!*"

"Duh!" says Paperstar. "I'm a *criminal.* And right now, I'm thinking that you and I should pull off the greatest art heist in history. Sounds like fun, right?"

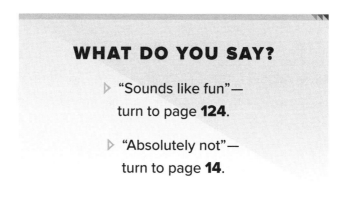

WHAT DO YOU SAY?

▷ "Sounds like fun"—
turn to page **124**.

▷ "Absolutely not"—
turn to page **14**.

"LET ME TALK TO THEM," you say. "I'll try to convince them not to take off."

"What are you going to tell them?" Ivy asks nervously.

"I don't know," you reply. "I'll think of something on the way."

And so, you walk across the concrete parking area between the two jets, butterflies in your stomach. When you get close to the Zeta Circuits jet, the cabin door swings open and Paperstar steps out.

"Can I help you?" she asks, in a voice that sounds both bored and mocking.

"I work at Zeta Circuits," you say. "Our elite security team has learned that the thief from last night was actually Carmen Sandiego. We think that she may be tracking your jet somehow."

Paperstar sighs loudly. "I need to make a call," she says, tapping a button on a video screen on her wrist.

"What is it, Paperstar?" says someone from the video screen.

"Trouble, Dr. Bellum," Paperstar replies. "Turns out that Carmen Sandiego is tracking our jet."

"That is unfortunate," says Bellum. "We'll have to transport the jetpacks by ship instead. Don't go any-where. I'm sending another operative to pick up the jet-packs now."

Paperstar taps the video screen on her wrist to end the call, then looks back at you. "You can go now," she says coldly.

When you get back to your own jet, Carmen grins and claps you on the shoulder. "Well played," she says. "It sounds like we'll have a chance to swipe those jet-packs after all."

Zack and Ivy go into the airport to rent a car, while you and Carmen wait and watch. An hour later, a green car approaches across the concrete. A VILE guard moves the crate with the jetpacks from the Zeta Circuits jet into the green car, and then the car drives away.

"Time to move," says Carmen. You race through the airport to the passenger pickup area, where Zack is wait-ing for you in an enormous SUV, almost like a monster truck, with tires half as tall as you are.

"He asked for the coolest safari truck they had," Ivy explains.

You and Carmen get in the back seat of the SUV, and Zack starts driving. Carmen puts Player on speakerphone. "Player," she says, "we saw VILE load the jetpacks into a green car. Can you track them?"

"I have them on security cameras leaving the airport, headed south," Player replies. *"They said they were moving the jetpacks by ship, right?"*

"That's right," you confirm.

"Nairobi isn't on the ocean," Player tells you. *"The main port city in Kenya is Mombasa, almost three hundred miles southeast of where you are now. There's one main*

highway between the two cities. I bet VILE is headed that way."

You find yourself outside the city of Nairobi driving through the Kenyan plains. Golden grassland stretches out in every direction, dotted with green acacia trees.

"I SPY A GIRAFFE!" Ivy shouts, jumping up in her seat. Sure enough, far to your left, you see a giraffe stretching its long neck to eat from the top of a tree. "They look even taller in person. That's one point for me!"

"I SPY THINGS WITH HORNS!" Zack yells. "And look there are like twenty of them, so that's twenty points for me."

"Those are impalas," you explain, recognizing them from nature documentaries. "They're a kind of antelope that travels in herds—known for being great jumpers."

"I SPY VILE!" says Carmen. "Do I get a point for that?" She points out a green car far ahead along the highway.

Zack guns the engine, and your monster SUV zooms forward, passing a van and a pickup truck to get closer to the VILE car. The VILE car speeds up too. "I think they see us," Zack says.

"Of course they see us," says Ivy. "We're driving the most obvious vehicle in all of Africa. We might as well be riding a rhinoceros."

The VILE car turns abruptly onto a dirt side road. Zack hits the brakes and your enormous tires squeal across the pavement as you turn to follow. The dirt road leads deeper into the wilderness, through rocks and scrubby bushes.

"I SPY A ZEBRA!" Zack shouts. "Point for me."

"Zack, focus!" says Carmen. As the road bends, you are right behind the VILE car. Zack cuts across the grass to get ahead of them, and then slams the brakes, spinning to face them. The car lurches off the road toward the edge of a watering hole, and then stops as its wheel sinks into the mud.

Carmen vaults out of the SUV, ready for action. You, Zack, and Ivy follow.

A VILE guard steps out of the front seat of his car, flexing his hands into fists. And then the back door swings open—and a mime steps out onto the grass. He is wearing a gray and black striped shirt and a black beret, with full white makeup covering his face. He also has large silver sneakers with thick soles that make him three inches taller.

"Mime Bomb!" says Carmen. "New shoes?"

The mime gives an elaborate bow. All six of you stare at each other under the hot Kenyan sun, Mime Bomb and the VILE guard on one side, you and Carmen's crew on the other. A nearby group of impalas glance up curiously and then return to munching the grass.

Mime Bomb holds up one finger, as if he's about to give a performance. Lifting his hat, he pulls out a silver ball. Then he curls his hands in front of him, like a baseball pitcher getting ready to throw. With an exaggerated windmill wind-up, he flings the ball right toward you.

On instinct, you reach out and catch the ball. It's

made of metal, perfectly smooth, and it vibrates in your hands with a dull hum.

"Crackle ball!" Carmen shouts.

WHAT DO YOU DO?

▷ If you throw the ball back at Mime Bomb, turn to page **138**.

▷ If you throw it into the watering hole, turn to page **31**.

"I DON'T KNOW WHAT I'll do with the jet-pack," you say. "Maybe just keep it as a souvenir."

You ask Carmen, Zack, and Ivy if they want to get dinner to celebrate your victory over VILE. You suggest your favorite dim sum place, just a few blocks away. An hour later, you are laughing over enormous plates 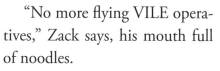 of salted egg custard buns and prawn dumplings.

"No more flying VILE operatives," Zack says, his mouth full of noodles.

"VILE is bad enough on the ground," Ivy agrees.

After dinner, you hug each of them goodbye and go home to your apartment, where you give the leftovers to your cat, Mustard. "Well, Mustard," you say, "looks like my big adventure is over. I'm going to need a new job."

There are lots of opportunities for an engineer like you in Singapore, and within a couple of weeks, you get a good job at a company that makes smart toasters that text you when your toast is done.

One day, you are looking through your closet for something clean to wear, when you see the jetpack hanging among your clothes. You haven't thought about it for months, but now you remember how exciting it was to fly. Your apartment has a tiny balcony that overlooks an alleyway between buildings. That night, you strap on the jetpack, pull on the control glove, and take off into the sky.

Invisible in the dark, you fly along the side of your apartment building, past the lit windows with people inside having dinner or watching TV. Turning higher, you soar over the rooftops, until you can see the Singapore Strait in the distance, crowded with the lights of cargo ships. You glide away from the city and over the beachfront paths of East Coast Park.

And then you hear a distant shout, like someone in trouble. You get lower and hear the shout again, someone yelling, "Help!" Spiraling toward the park, you see a person in a hooded sweatshirt running along the beach, shouting for help again and again, until a large man tackles him from behind.

The man raises his fist to strike. Almost without thinking, you dive down and grab him by the back of his shirt, and then arc back into the air, carrying him with you. The man hollers as you fly out over the ocean and drop him into the shallow water.

In the weeks that follow, you start regularly patrolling the parks and other dark corners of the city at night. You chase down a purse-snatcher and break up a mugging. Remembering the Zeta Circuits security drones, you brew some of the same fast-drying liquid goo that they used, along with a portable squirter that you can take with you when you fly. You use the stuff to freeze criminals.

People in Singapore start to tell stories about a mysterious person who swooped from the sky to help them when they were in trouble. You feel like a superhero in a comic book. You never see Carmen Sandiego again, but you are proud that, just like her, you are using your powers to fight for good.

THE END

"I'M SORRY," YOU SAY. "I love my job, and I've already done too much. I need to get to work."

"*I understand,*" says Player. "*Thanks, anyway. And good luck.*"

When you arrive at the Zeta Circuits building, twenty minutes late, everyone is talking about the theft. How did the thieves get to a twenty-ninth-story window? How did they hack the security cameras in the vault to make it look like the jetpack was there the whole time?

The security team knows that you were in the building at the time of the robbery. You lie to them, saying that you fell asleep at your desk and missed the whole thing. They seem to believe you.

Although one jetpack was stolen, three more were delivered to your client, and your boss tells you that the client is pleased. To celebrate, Zeta Circuits throws a party on Sentosa, a resort island on the southern edge of the city. You laugh with your coworkers, enjoying the delicious food and drink, and not thinking at all about Carmen Sandiego.

You get assigned to a new project—a drone attached

to a leash that can take a dog for a walk without needing a person.

A couple of weeks later, you hear about a strange crime. A luxury yacht was hijacked in the middle of the Coral Sea, off the east coast of Australia. The captain, who was the only one onboard, claims that the thieves flew out of the sky.

You remember Carmen's warning about VILE and flying thieves. Is it possible that VILE stole the yacht using the jetpacks that you helped build? Maybe. Or maybe the captain was delusional, or maybe he was working with the thieves and made up the story.

You will never know.

THE END

"I'M SORRY," you tell Paperstar. "I'm responsible for delivering these jetpacks to Reykjavik, and I'm not allowed to change plans."

Paperstar snatches back the paper doll she made for you and, with a flick of her thumb, pops off its head. "In that case," she sneers, "I suggest we spend the rest of our flight in uncomfortable silence."

When you arrive at Reykjavik Airport, you, Paperstar, and the crate with the jetpacks are transferred to a helicopter with a V-shaped logo on the side. As you lift off, you ask the helicopter pilot where you are going, but she shakes her head. "Location is classified. You'll find out when you get there."

Paperstar is still ignoring you, so you decide to ignore her, too, and enjoy the scenery. You spot the crater of an old volcano beneath you—Iceland has about two hundred volcanoes, and about a tenth of the country's land was made from cooled lava. You remind yourself to come back here someday when you have more time to explore.

After a few hours, the helicopter approaches a high plateau, surrounded by cliffs that plunge down into the

ocean. This is one of Iceland's famous fjords, U-shaped valleys cut inland from the ocean by ancient glaciers.

On top of the plateau stands a small metal building with an enormous antenna sticking out the top. As the helicopter touches down, you see a small woman in a lab coat, with a shock of white hair and a wild grin on her face.

"Welcome to Iceland," she proclaims, her arms open wide.

"Dr. Bellum," says Paperstar lazily, "I'm surprised to see you away from headquarters."

"The life of science is full of surprises," Bellum replies. "This mission is so important that I have decided to supervise it in person. In any case, Paperstar, you should be honored that I have chosen you to be part of my elite squad of flying operatives . . . *the Soaring Bellums!*"

"We are not calling ourselves that," Paperstar grumbles.

"And you must be the engineer from Zeta Circuits," Bellum says, turning to you. "Are you ready to give us a flying lesson?"

"Of course," you reply. "Ready when you are."

"Excellent," says Bellum. "Here come the rest of our fliers."

Two men walk toward you from the metal building. The first one, tall with a goatee, introduces himself as Le Chèvre. The second, very thin and wearing a black jumpsuit, calls himself Neal the Eel. You unload the jetpacks from the crate and give one each to the two men, and the third to Paperstar.

Le Chèvre looks uncomfortable as he straps on the plastic backpack. "Le Chèvre is already a master of heights," he complains. "I do not need a flying toy that will most likely break at the worst possible time."

"Silence!" snaps Bellum. "All of you, listen and learn."

You explain that each jetpack is paired with a control glove that you wear on your right hand. The jetpack responds to your hand gestures: thumbs-up to start the engine, tilt your palm to steer, make a fist to stop.

Paperstar shoots up into the air, then falls

straight down, stopping herself to hover about fifteen feet in the air. Neal and then Le Chèvre take off too, matching her height.

Bellum cheers. "Outstanding!" she says. "Now let's try a challenge." She goes into the building and returns with a bouquet of balloons in different colors. When Bellum lets the balloons go, they scatter into the sky, drifting past the edge of the cliff to float high over the ocean.

"Whoever catches the most balloons," she says to her operatives, "will be named squad leader of the Soaring Bellums. On your marks. Get set. Go!"

On *go,* the three operatives start their jetpacks and shoot toward the balloons. Paperstar shoves Neal the Eel as they lift off, sending him flailing sideways. Le Chèvre, a few feet ahead of the others, twists gracefully in the air and grabs the nearest balloon.

"Just look at them," Bellum says to you. "Ask any child what superpower they would choose, and you will get the same answer: *I wish I could fly.* It's even better than laser eye beams."

"They're getting good," you say. In the distance, Paperstar snatches a balloon inches from Le Chèvre's fingertips, while Neal the Eel chases a stray so high that it's only a red dot against the blue sky.

"Indeed," Bellum says. "The jetpacks work better

than I hoped. I will tell your superiors at Zeta Circuits that we accept the delivery and will send the full payment."

"That's great news," you say. "I'm curious—why did we come all the way out to the fjords to test the jetpacks? There's nothing but rocks and ocean, and that one little building."

"Ah," says Bellum proudly. "What you see is only the tip of the iceberg. There is an enormous workshop carved into the rock beneath our feet. In fact, my people here are working on a giant robbing robot right now."

She must be kidding. "Did you say 'giant robbing robot'?"

"Oh yes," she says, rubbing her hands together gleefully. "My robot will be strong enough to punch through meta't matter what I tell you," she says. "We're going to erase your memory before you leave here. I obviously can't let you know the location of my secret laboratory."

"What? I don't want my memory erased!"

"Oh, don't worry!" Bellum says with a friendly chuckle. "The memory-wiping helmet will be carefully targeted. You will forget your visit to Iceland and nothing else."

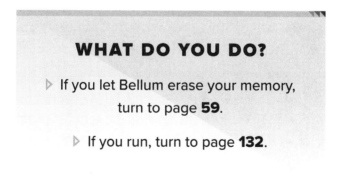

WHAT DO YOU DO?

▷ If you let Bellum erase your memory, turn to page **59**.

▷ If you run, turn to page **132**.

REALIZING THAT PAPERSTAR is danger-
ous, you sprint down the hall in the other direction,
leaving her and the guards behind. You need to find a
quick exit from the museum so that you can put this
whole night behind you.

You come into another large room full of marble
sculptures, many showing people in scenes of battle or
agony. You notice one of Hercules, the hero of Greek
mythology, battling a centaur. You wish that you were
here as a regular tourist so that you could spend more
time looking at the art.

A group of guards charge into the room from a different hallway. You make a hand gesture and your jetpack whirs to life, lifting you above the shouting guards.
You zoom upward, over Hercules's head, toward an
arched skylight that covers the room.

Too fast. You almost collide with the glass before you
cut the power to dip back toward the ground. A guard
leaps up, grabbing you by both feet. *Oh no!* You push the
jetpack back to full power, dragging the guard up into the
air with you, but a second guard jumps up and also grabs
your ankle—too much weight for the jetpack to handle.

They drag you down to the ground and surround you, electric rods pointing at you.

"You are under arrest," one of them says.

During your trial, you learn that your partner—Paperstar—escaped with the painting *Musical Angel*. The judge sentences you to twenty years in prison, telling you that you're worse than a common thief because when you steal great art, you steal from every person in the entire world.

How did you go from being a successful engineer in Singapore to a criminal in Florence in just a few days? Well, now you'll have plenty of time to think about your mistakes.

THE END

FOR ALL YOU KNOW, Carmen Sandiego may be here to steal the jewels herself. Your best bet is to avoid her.

You move through the crowd to the far side of the room, feeling out of place even though no one is paying attention to you. Agent Zari walks up next to you and says casually, "VILE has an operative at the party. Do you see that young woman in the red dress? Don't look!"

"You mean Carmen Sandiego?" you ask. "She's not—"

"Ladies and gentlemen!" booms a voice from across the room. "Does anyone here like *jewels?*" The speaker is a large man with a bushy mustache, wearing a silver tuxedo. "Follow me out onto the balcony. The auction is about to begin."

"I can hardly wait," Zari whispers sarcastically in your ear.

The wide balcony is surrounded by a glass wall, taller than a person. Night has fallen, and the lights of Dubai sparkle far beneath you. Ten marble pedestals are lined up against the glass wall, blocked off by a velvet rope from the rest the balcony. On top of each pedestal rests a silver case, which must contain the jewels up for auction.

The man in the silver tuxedo opens the first case and dramatically lifts out a diamond necklace, each stone the size of a walnut. "The story of this necklace," he says, "begins in the year 1905, when the Cullinan Diamond was discovered in a mine in South Africa. Weighing more than a pound, it was the largest diamond ever found and was carved into more than one hundred separate gemstones."

"Carmen Sandiego is gone," Zari whispers in your ear. You scan the crowd for a red dress and, sure enough, she's not there.

The crowd presses closer while the man continues his story. "This priceless necklace is made entirely of diamonds carved from that original Cullinan Diamond, each gemstone sparkling with history!" He goes on to talk about each individual stone, their weight and quality, but you're not paying attention. You look around for Carmen.

The man puts the diamond necklace back in its case and moves on to the second pedestal. "Night has fallen," he says, gesturing toward the view through the glass wall. "It's time for the stars to come out!" he declares. "Or in our case, a *star sapphire!*"

As he reaches to open the second case, something like hail falls from the sky, bunches of small pebbles that bounce off the guests and scatter on the ground. A moment later, each pebble explodes in a puff, filling the air with colored smoke.

Three shadowy figures glide down onto the balcony through the smoke, landing among the pedestals with the jewels. *VILE is here!* One of them, a tall man with a beard, grabs the case with the diamond necklace.

Agent Zari charges out of the crowd and tackles the man, sending the silver case flying through the air and over the glass wall at the edge of the balcony. People start to scream and run, losing their way in the smoke and slamming into one another.

A second VILE operative dips down to grab two more jewel cases, and then hovers above the crowd. "Sweet party," she gloats, "sorry we gotta jet."

A red triangular shape dives toward the VILE operative from above. Rubbing your eyes, you see that it's Carmen Sandiego on a red hang glider. She must have glided down from a higher floor! Carmen tackles the VILE operative in the air and pulls off her jetpack, sending her tumbling to the balcony.

Moving fast, you yank off the VILE operative's

control glove—the glove works like a remote control for the jetpack—and slip it on your own hand. You make a gesture telling her jetpack to come to you. Sure enough, it flies through the air on its own, right into your hands. You strap the jetpack onto your back and take off into the night sky.

As alarm bells clang, you soar above the smoky confusion of the party. You spot the third VILE operative flying away, carrying two of the silver cases with the jewels inside. He's a tall, thin man in a black jumpsuit.

Following him over the glass wall, you look down at the city below. You're not usually afraid of heights, but your stomach lurches as you see the bright tops of smaller skyscrapers pointing up at you.

Shaking off your fear, you follow the VILE operative, who is barely visible in the moonlight. He turns toward the ocean—maybe meeting up with a ship. You're both going full speed, so you're not able to get any closer, and you worry that you'll lose your target in the darkness.

But the jetpacks do have an experimental "turbo boost" that makes the engines fire at super speed for a few seconds. Unfortunately, you can't steer during a turbo boost, and occasionally during testing, it caused the jetpacks to explode.

WHAT DO YOU DO?

▷ If you fly normally, turn to page **40**.

▷ If you turbo boost, turn to page **65**.

"SHE DIDN'T TELL ME ANYTHING,"

you say. "I've never heard of Carmen Sandiego."

Zari looks at you with suspicion. "I don't believe you," she says, "and I don't want you on my operation. Leave now—or I'll call the police to have you arrested."

Reluctantly, you take the elevator down to the ground floor and exit onto the streets of Dubai. Looking up at the Burj Khalifa, a spear of light that goes impossibly far into the sky, you wonder what is happening up on the balcony of the 112th floor. Did VILE try to steal the jewels? Did Carmen stop them? You may never know.

Suddenly, something smashes onto the ground, just a few feet from where you are standing. It shatters violently and cracks the sidewalk.

Looking closer, you see that it is one of the silver cases from the jewel auction. And there, lying at your feet, is a spectacular diamond necklace, gems the size of walnuts strung together with silver. The necklace feels surprisingly heavy when you pick it up, the diamonds sparkling brilliantly in the streetlights. You slip it into your pocket.

The next day, you look for stories online about what

happened. There's nothing about a robbery, but you do see a story that a precious diamond necklace was lost at the Burj Khalifa. The owner is offering a $100,000 reward if it is safely returned, with no questions asked. You smile to yourself. Although you weren't able to stop VILE, this could be a very happy ending for you.

YOU LOOK UP THE NUMBER for Sal's Pizza in Niagara Falls, Canada. With a deep breath, you press the button to make the call.

"Sal's Pizza," says a voice on the other end. *"The finest slice at any price."* The voice sounds young, like a teenage boy.

"Is Carmen there?" you ask.

"I think you have the wrong number," says the boy.

"I mean . . . I'd like to order a pizza for delivery, please. One Buenos Aires Special."

"An excellent choice," he says. *"We've been hoping to hear from you. You can call me Player. I'm a friend of Carmen's."*

"Please," you say. "I'm in trouble." You peek out to see the three agents coming down the street toward you. "A bunch of people in black suits and sunglasses are following me. They must be from VILE."

"They're not VILE," Player says. *"We've met them before, though, and they are definitely trouble. Hang tight and I'll get you out of there. Locking on to your location . . ."*

You hear the clacking of computer keys through the phone. One of the agents spots you and points, and then all three of them dash toward your hiding spot. "Please hurry!" you say desperately as you start to run.

"There's a fancy jewelry store across the street from you," Player says. *"Go in there."*

Sure enough, you see a jewelry store right across the street, the kind of place where only the richest of the rich come to shop, with jeweled bracelets and other treasures sparkling in the window. You dash across the street through the double doors.

The moment that you get inside the jewelry store, a loud alarm goes off. Wealthy customers and salespeople look up in surprise as a heavy metal gate drops with a **CLANG,** blocking the doors behind you. The three agents slam into the gate, rattling the metal in frustration.

"How did you do that?" you gasp into the phone.

"I'm a white-hat hacker," Player says proudly. *"I've got lots of tricks. There's a side door across the main showroom. Everything is locked down right now, but I'm going to open it for you in three . . . two . . . one . . ."*

You sprint across the showroom, dodging glass cases full of sparkling stones, to the side door. The moment you arrive, you hear the click of a lock and push the door open.

"That should buy you a couple of minutes," Player says. *"There's a Mass Rapid Transit station half a block from you*

and a train arriving in . . . ninety seconds. If you run, you can catch it."

You run and, sure enough, you arrive on the platform just as the train doors are closing. You dodge inside, safe for the moment. You realize, though, that it won't be long until the agents in black find you again.

You've been wanting to start a new life. Maybe this is your chance. You make a quick stop at home to get your cat, Mustard, and your passport. Then you head straight to the airport, where you book the next flight for San Francisco, a perfect city for a high-tech engineer like you.

You hope that someday you will meet Carmen Sandiego again, and that next time, you can help her the way that she helped you.

THE END

"STOP THE ENGINES FOR NOW," you say. "We don't want any trouble with the police."

Zack pulls back the throttle to stop the *Narwhal*'s engines. You race out onto the deck, where Carmen is crouched behind the railing, watching the ocean behind you through a pair of binoculars. You can see the ship that is chasing you as a distant speck.

"That ship just radioed us and ordered us to stop," you tell her. "They say they're the police."

"They're not regular police," Carmen says, handing you the binoculars. You scan the ocean until you are able to focus on the ship. It's long and sleek, painted black from bow to stern. On deck, you see two people who look like secret agents, dressed in black suits and sunglasses.

"Those are strange clothes for boating," you say. "Who are they?"

"I don't know exactly," Carmen says. "They followed me in Paris a while back. They definitely know my face, and they might recognize Zack and Ivy too. Player says they're faster than we are, so when they get here, you need to talk to them."

Carmen, Zack, and Ivy hide in the cabin while you wait for the mysterious black ship. As it gets closer, you

see a name on the hull: *Gumshoe*, an unusual name for an unusual ship. A voice blares on a loudspeaker across the water. "You there! Are you alone?"

You nod and give the thumbs-up.

"We're sending over a raft," the voice says. "You need to come with us right now."

An agent lowers a motorized raft into the ocean, and then drives over to the *Narwhal*. You climb a ladder on the outside of your hull to get down to the raft, and then ride across the choppy water to the *Gumshoe*.

When you get up on deck, one of the agents greets you. "I'm Agent Zari," she says. "What are you doing out here?"

"I'm sailing around the world," you lie. "I started in Singapore, cut south through the Java Sea, quick stop in Australia to stock up, and now I'm zipping across the Pacific to the Panama Canal."

"Who else is on your ship?" she asks.

"I'm alone. For me, the sea and sky are the best company."

"Uh-huh," Zari says, sounding skeptical. "We're in a hurry, so I'll get to the point. Right now, I'm chasing a group of thieves, probably the most dangerous criminals in the world. This might be our best chance to catch them in years."

Interesting. It sounds like they're also chasing VILE. Maybe Carmen and this Agent Zari are on the same side.

"If you know anything, anything at all, that can help us," Zari says, "you should tell me now."

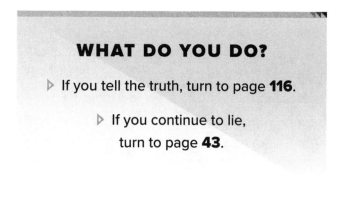

WHAT DO YOU DO?

▷ If you tell the truth, turn to page **116**.

▷ If you continue to lie,
turn to page **43**.

YOU TAKE BELLUM'S HAND. "I'll stick with the good team," you say. Firing your jetpack engines, you lift her over the railing of her ship and drop her into the ocean.

Zack throws life preservers to Le Chèvre, Paperstar, Neal the Eel, and Bellum, all of them now bobbing in the ocean. Meanwhile, Ivy boards the VILE ship and disables the engines and the communications. Once the

VILE crew climbs back aboard their ship, they have no way to go anywhere.

As you sail away, Carmen calls Player. "That ship that was chasing us before—can you send them a message?"

"*Of course,*" says Player on the speakerphone. "*In fact, they just got their navigation systems back online and are heading toward you now.*"

Carmen grins. "Tell them that there's a VILE ship waiting for them, dead in the water. I think they'll be very interested in Dr. Bellum and her crew."

"Wow," says Zack. "Did we really just get a VILE mastermind busted?"

"I think we did," Carmen says. "This will be a huge blow, much bigger than stopping their jetpack crew. It will take them years to recover."

"So, what now?" you ask.

"We're already heading to Fiji," Carmen says, smiling at you. "Let's keep going. We've all earned a sweet vacation." You smile back and feel like part of the crew.

THE END

YOU DECIDE TO STICK with Paperstar. "Hold my painting," she says, handing it to you.

One of the guards steps forward, holding the electric rod in front of him. "There's no way out," he says. "Come quietly and you won't get hurt."

Paperstar pulls a sheet of paper from her pouch, which she folds into a dart and flings at the guard. "Ow!" he howls, dropping his electric rod as the dart hits his hand.

A second guard charges, electric rod ready to strike. Paperstar braids three sheets of paper into what looks like a short rope, which she flings at the guard's feet. The paper rope wraps around the guard's ankles, tangling them together. The guard trips and slides along the polished marble floor, crashing into a wall.

The third guard's eyes go wide. She thinks for a moment and then sprints in the opposite direction, shouting into her phone for backup.

"Do you want to steal some more stuff?" Paperstar asks. "Or do you think we should go?"

"I think we should go," you say.

The two of you walk back into the gallery with the broken skylight, turn on your jetpacks, and take off into the Florence night. As you rise over the roof of the Uffizi, you hear sirens and see police cars approaching from all directions. They'll surround the building, but you doubt that anyone will look to the sky.

"That was fun," says Paperstar. "What do you want to steal next? I hear that France has some great stuff."

You and Paperstar become partners in crime, best friends, and flying thieves. You figure out that it's easy to steal from penthouse apartments—people who live on the fiftieth floor don't lock their balconies, and they often leave valuable things lying around. Sometimes for a bigger challenge, you strike a museum or an art gallery. Your engineering skills come in handy when you need to get past a security system.

You become rich, very rich, and get an enormous apartment for the two of you in Singapore (on the top floor, of course). There's no way to sell all the famous artwork you steal, so you keep it around the apartment.

You have Monet's *Bridge over a Pond of Water Lilies* hanging in your living room, a Picasso sculpture next to the bath, and in the kitchen, an ancient Greek vase that you use to hold fruit.

THE END

"YOU SHOULD STEAL the prototype jetpack," you tell Carmen. "But I can help."

Most of Singapore is on one main island, but there are also about sixty smaller islands that are part of the city. Zeta Circuits has a storage building on one of these islands, which is where the only remaining jetpack is being kept.

You know that the island has extremely high security, so you help Carmen make a plan. She will use scuba gear to get to the island. Once she's there, she can use your security code to get in the back door of the storage building.

Two nights later, you are in Singapore's East Coast Park, waiting for Carmen to return from the mission. Zack and Ivy are waiting with you, sitting on a park bench at the edge of the ocean. You check the time on your phone. Carmen has been gone for eighty-five minutes.

"Doesn't this drive you crazy?" you ask Zack and Ivy. "Waiting like this while Carmen is on a caper, with no idea whether she's okay?"

"Well, we do bring snacks," Zack says, offering you a bag of chips.

"Plus, Carm's a pro. I'm sure she's okay," Ivy reassures you.

Seconds later, you hear a splash at the edge of the water, and Carmen climbs out, dripping wet in her rubber wetsuit. She's opens a waterproof bag and pulls out the prototype jetpack.

"How was it?" Ivy asks.

"Medium challenge," Carmen says. "There are floodlights all over the island, which made it hard to find a place to come ashore. And then the door had a retinal scanner, so Player had to do some emergency hacking."

"All in a day's thieving," Zack says merrily. "Did the jetpack self-destruct yet?"

"There's no self-destruct on the prototype," you say. "It was never supposed to leave the building."

You hear a buzz and look up to see three metal balls floating over your head, each with a large camera eye and a nozzle sticking out the front. *Stop thieves,* one of them booms in a robotic voice.

"Security drones!" you shout. "They must be tracking the jetpack."

One of the drones shoots a

green liquid out of its nozzle at Zack. He tries to dodge, but the liquid soaks his legs and he falls over. You realize that his legs are frozen in position—the liquid has hardened instantly into a shell. You remember hearing about a fast-freezing goo that another division of Zeta Circuits was working on, but you didn't know that it was finished, or that it was so effective.

A second drone turns its nozzle toward you. Carmen lifts her arm and shoots a grappling hook at the drone, then yanks the rope with all her strength, smashing the drone into the ground. The broken drone sparks and whirs as it tries to fly again.

The third drone fires green liquid at Carmen, catching her still-outstretched arms and freezing them in front of her. In this fight, you'll have a better chance in the air. You put on the prototype jetpack that Carmen just stole. A compartment on the side of the jetpack holds a control glove, which you use like a remote control to tell the jetpack what to do. Slipping the glove on your right hand, you make a gesture to take off into the air.

Both remaining drones spin toward you and fire green goo, but you are moving too fast and streak past them, getting above them. Making a quick adjustment, you loop back behind one of the drones and grab it with both hands like a basketball. Streaking forward, you drive the one drone into the other. They collide with a shower of sparks, and then both fall to the ground.

You land next to Carmen, whose arms are still stuck out in front of her. "That was some sweet flying," she says. "Any idea how I can move again?"

"It's not permanent," you say. "In fact, the shell dissolves in salt water!" Carmen jumps back into the ocean. When she comes out, she can move her arms again, peeling bits of green goo off her wetsuit.

"What about me?" Zack pleads from the ground, pointing to his frozen legs. "This is getting uncomfortable."

"We'll come back for you tomorrow," Ivy jokes. Then she drags Zack to the edge of the water and tips him in. He splashes while the shell around his legs dissolves, and then gets shakily to his feet.

"You're a good flier," Carmen says to you. "What are you going to do with that jetpack?"

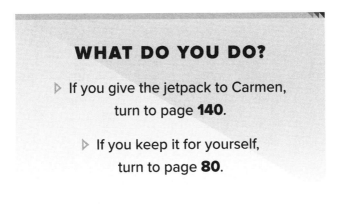

WHAT DO YOU DO?

▷ If you give the jetpack to Carmen,
turn to page **140**.

▷ If you keep it for yourself,
turn to page **80**.

YOU DECIDE TO TELL Agent Zari the truth. "My friends and I are chasing VILE too. We should work together."

"Your friends?" Zari asks suspiciously. "You said you were alone with the sea and sky."

"I'm traveling with Carmen Sandiego," you admit.

At the mention of the name Carmen Sandiego, Zari's eyes go wide. She presses her earpiece and starts talking. "Chief! This is Zari. We found a ship with Carmen Sandiego onboard. What are your orders?" Zari nods as she listens to someone in her earpiece telling her what to do. "All agents!" she calls. "We're storming the *Narwhal*! Look for a woman in red and take her prisoner!"

Oh no! You run to the railing of the *Gumshoe*. "*Carmen!*" you shout across the water, as loud as you can. "Get out of here! They're coming for you!"

The *Narwhal*'s engines roar to life, and it starts to move, pushing through the waves. "Stop that ship!" Zari shouts. "Launch the EMP torpedo! And lock this one in the brig," she says, pointing to you.

Someone grabs you from behind. You are led roughly into the ship's cabin and down a flight of stairs, where you are pushed inside a small, windowless room with a couple of benches bolted to the wall. You kick the door as hard as you can, but it's too strong. "Let me out of here!" you yell.

You wait for what seems like forever, and then the door opens, and Zack and Ivy are shoved into the room. "What happened?" you ask frantically.

"We were gonna get away," says Zack, "and then our engines just died."

"I think it was an EMP," says Ivy. "That's like a burst of energy that kills any electrical system. They must've hit us with one somehow."

"Where's Carmen?" you ask.

Zack shrugs his shoulders. "They said they were taking her to talk to someone called Chief. I'm sure she'll be okay, though. Carm always wins in the end."

But if Carmen does win in the end, you never find out. You are taken to Brisbane, Australia, where you are locked in a windowless room and interviewed again and again. The agents want to know about VILE, about the jetpacks, and, most of all, about Carmen Sandiego. They think that Carmen is involved somehow with VILE, or that she may even be the secret leader of VILE. Nothing you say convinces them otherwise.

When they finally let you go, you fly back to Singapore, thinking about what you should do next.

You don't know what happened to Carmen, or to Zack and Ivy, and feel terrible that you gave them up. You hope that, somehow, they will be okay.

AN HOUR LATER, you are at Changi Airport, walking across the tarmac toward a private jet. When you step into the cabin, a young man with orange hair leaps up to meet you. "Finally!" he booms. "Our food delivery is here!"

"I told you," says a freckled woman. "They don't deliver to the runway." She reaches out to shake your hand. "My name is Ivy," she says, "and this is my brother, Zack. You must be the engineer who worked on the jet-packs, right?"

"Yes," you say, shaking Ivy's hand. "That's me."

Carmen Sandiego sits cross-legged on her seat, typing on a laptop computer. "I'm glad you came," she says to you. "Player, please tell the pilot that we're all here and ready to take off."

"Sure thing, Red," says Player's voice, coming from the laptop. *"Buckle your seat belts, and no moving around the cabin."*

You choose a seat and buckle up. "Player isn't with you?" you ask.

"No," says Ivy. "Player works from home. He may be an all-star hacker, but his mom still likes him to be home for dinner."

"So where are we going again?" you ask, once the jet is in the air.

"Nairobi," says Player from Carmen's laptop. *"It's the capital of Kenya in East Africa. Kenya is home to about 50 million people, along with elephants, cheetahs, giraffes, lions, rhinoceroses—"*

"You hear that, bro!" says Ivy. "Sounds like we're going on a real-life safari!"

"Let's play a safari challenge," Zack says. "Whoever sees the most animals wins."

"Deal," Ivy exclaims. "But we only count animals that we could never see in the wild in Boston. So, no pigeons or stuff like that."

"First we have some jetpacks to steal," says Carmen. "And then . . . yeah, I would totally love to see a giraffe."

The flight takes more than nine hours, as you cross the Indian Ocean. You touch down in Nairobi under a hot afternoon sun. You taxi from the runway to the

terminal where the private jets park—and see another jet parked a few hundred feet away.

"We're in luck!" you say. "That's the Zeta Circuits jet! It's still here!"

"Let's steal those jetpacks!" says Zack. "Carm, do your thing!"

Carmen shakes her head. "I'm a thief, not a magician," she says. "Even I can't break into a private jet in a busy airport in broad daylight."

"Hey, guys," says Ivy. "Someone's coming."

Sure enough, a young woman in stylish, colorful clothing is walking across the tarmac. "I know her from school," Carmen says. "Her name is Paperstar."

Paperstar climbs aboard the Zeta Circuits jet. *"Uh-oh,"* says Player. *"They just got cleared for takeoff. They haven't filed a flight plan, so I don't know where they're going next. Once they take off, they're gone."*

"We're so close!" says Carmen with frustration.

Zack puts a hand on your shoulder. "You work for Zeta Circuits, right? Maybe you could tell the jet not to take off."

"Why would they listen to me?" you ask. "I'm not even supposed to be here!"

"I don't know," Zack replies sheepishly. "Make up a story or something."

WHAT DO YOU SAY?

▷ If you try to convince the Zeta Circuits jet not to take off, turn to page **73**.

▷ If you let them go for now, turn to page **16**.

"SOUNDS LIKE FUN," you say.

"Best thieves forever," says Paperstar, flying down through the hole in the skylight and landing on the floor. You're in a gallery full of statues. "These look heavy," she says. "Let's find some more portable artwork."

You follow her down a hall with paintings on either side, beautiful images of saints and nobles, created by some of art's greatest masters. "Do you see any that you like?" Paperstar asks.

"I like all of them," you say, wondering already if you've made a mistake.

She settles in front of a small painting of a cherub play-

ing a lute. "*Musical Angel* by Rosso Fiorentino," she reads. "This one is cute." She reaches for it.

"Wait! You'll set off the alarm—"

The moment that Paperstar pulls the painting off the wall, a siren blares, echoing through the marble halls of the museum. "Time to fly," says Paperstar, dashing back the way you came with the painting tucked under her arm.

Three guards step out from a side hall, blocking your path. They are armed with metal rods that crackle with electricity—some sort of stun device, you guess.

"Quick! Let's go the other way!" you shout.

"No need," says Paperstar, her voice as calm as ever. "I'm about to give an art history lesson. As in, this is *art* . . ." She holds up the painting she stole. "And the guards are *history.*"

WHAT DO YOU DO?

▷ If you run, turn to page **92**.

▷ If you stick with Paperstar, turn to page **109**.

"I'LL GET THE PROTOTYPE JETPACK,"

you say. "I should be able to walk right in the front door."

Most of Singapore is on one main island, but there are also about sixty smaller islands that are part of the city. Zeta Circuits has a high-security storage building on one of these islands, which is where the only remaining jetpack is being kept. In fact, Zeta Circuits owns the entire island, and the only way to get there is by a company ferry that goes back and forth from the mainland twice a day.

On a warm Tuesday morning, you step off the ferry and follow a stone path toward the high-security storage building. Along the path, you pass someone you know coming in the other direction and greet him with a friendly nod.

You walk through double doors at the front of the building, beneath a huge Zeta Circuits logo. A guard behind a desk waves you over, and you show him your ID card. He nods and asks you what you're doing there. "I'm on the jetpack team," you say. "I need to make a software update to the prototype."

"Sure thing," the guard says. He presses a button

under his desk, and a metal door swings open behind him. "Down the hall, door number nine."

Through the door, you walk down a brightly lit hall with numbered doors on either side, odds on the left, evens on the right. When you arrive at door number nine, it swings open by itself with a metallic click.

You enter a small room, with the jetpack prototype hanging on a mannequin and a large monitor on the wall. You remember when you found Carmen in your vault late at night and realize that now you're in the same situation, but this time you're the thief.

As you reach out to take the jetpack, the door to room number nine slams shut behind you and the monitor on the wall flashes on. Your boss from Zeta Circuits stares down at you, her face filling the screen. "We thought you might try something like this," she says.

"Something like what?" you ask. "I'm not trying anything. I just needed to check on the—"

"Don't bother lying," she says. "We know that you're working with the jetpack thief. We have pictures of you together at the airport in Nairobi."

"Okay," you admit. "I am working with her. But please believe me, we're the good guys. The people who are buying the jetpacks are *criminals*."

She waves you off. "The only criminal I see is you."

"Are you going to have me arrested?" you ask fearfully.

"No, we don't want the police involved in this. I'm giving you to our client, as an apology for the missing jetpacks."

Your boss disappears from the monitor and is replaced by a woman with round glasses and a shock of white hair. "My name is Dr. Saira Bellum," she introduces herself. "I understand that you have volunteered to test my new experimental mind-control device. Fabulous!"

"What? No! I didn't volunteer for anything."

"Hmm," she says, making notes on a tablet. "I see that you have a bad attitude. We'll have to adjust that. See you soon!" The screen goes dark.

THE END

"CARMEN WENT UP to a higher floor," you say. "She wants to get a view from above."

Zari presses a button on a hidden earpiece. "Chief," she says, "Carmen Sandiego has left the party. Did any elevators leave the 112th floor in the last minute, going up?" Zari nods, and then nods again, as she listens to Chief speak into her ear.

"The elevator's been tracked to 120," she tells you. "We have five agents in the building, moving in now. We should be able to catch her by surprise."

"You're making a mistake," you plead. "Carmen isn't here to steal the jewels. She's here to save the jewels."

"A thief is a thief," Zari says coldly, "and tonight we're going to catch a thief." She paces nervously as she listens to her earpiece, and then pumps both fists in the air. "We got her!" Zari whoops. The other partygoers turn to look. Zari smiles at them and says again, more quietly, "We got her."

A man in a silver tuxedo claps for attention at the other side of the room. "Ladies and gentlemen," he calls in a booming voice, "your attention, please! I have just learned of a plan to steal the jewels from our auction. Don't worry, the thief was caught, but as a precaution, we are canceling tonight's party. You all have my sincere apologies."

Grumbles fill the room as the guests mill toward the elevator. Zari talks quietly into your ear. "Check into a hotel," she tells you. "We'll be in touch soon."

You leave the Burj Khalifa and go to a hotel across the street. When you get to your room, you flop down on the bed, exhausted. How long has it been since you slept?

A shiny pen lies on the pillow next to you, just like the one Agent Zari had in Singapore. Sitting up in bed, you click it—then toss it to the floor as blue light pours out. The light forms into the figure of Chief, a shining hologram standing in the middle of the hotel room. "Nice room," she says, looking around. "Well, you've earned it."

"I didn't do anything," you say.

"You did everything," she insists. "We have been chasing Carmen Sandiego for months. You found her and gave us the tip we needed to finally catch her. Today you're more than an engineer. Today you're a hero."

Chief's hologram disappears. The truth is, you don't feel one bit like a hero. After all that happened, you believe that Carmen Sandiego was on the good side of things. You wish that she hadn't been caught—and you have a feeling that it's all your fault.

THE END

NOBODY IS GOING TO ERASE your memories. You need to get out of here—but how?

You notice a fishing boat on the ocean below. If you can get down there, maybe you can tell the captain what is happening and ask for help. You have to move quickly, though. All three VILE operatives are now chasing one distant balloon, and once they fly back, you'll have no chance to escape.

You dash toward the cliff. When you reach the rocky edge, you spot a path where the cliff is less steep, leading to a ledge about halfway down. Luckily, you aren't afraid of heights. Scrambling on all fours, you slide down a pebbled rockface and catch on to a boulder.

Bellum's head appears above you at the lip of the cliff. "Get back here!" she shouts, stomping her foot. "Why are you making such a fuss over a little memory cleanup?"

You swing off a rock that sticks out from the cliff face, dropping to a lower ledge, which is only about two feet wide. You're probably still too high to jump into the ocean, plus you aren't sure that you could clear the rocks. *Keep going.*

Hugging the rock wall with your body, you follow

the ledge down. It gets narrower and the rocks here are crumbly, so you're unsure of your footholds. As you stretch your right leg over a gap, the stones beneath your left foot give way. You spin outward from the ledge and lose your handhold, tumbling into open space, head over heels toward the rocks below.

Strong hands grab the back of your shirt. *Le Chèvre!* Hovering in the air, his jetpack engines firing at full strength, he pulls you upward. "You made me drop all my balloons," he mutters.

Le Chèvre drops you back on top of the cliff, where Bellum stands with crossed arms and a furious look. Paperstar and Neal the Eel hover over her head. "I see that you like to start trouble," Bellum says. "Now you will face the consequences."

"Please don't erase my memory," you plead.

"Oh, we're well beyond that," Bellum snaps. "I need moving targets to test my robot's laser eye beams. You'll be perfect for the job."

THE END

YOU PICK UP THE JETPACK and strap
it on your back. Carmen tosses you the control glove,
which you slip onto your right hand. A moment later,
you are in the air.

You arc away from the *Narwhal*, over the open ocean.
Le Chèvre and Neal the Eel follow you, one on either
side, getting closer. From their precise movements, you
can see that they've been practicing with the jetpacks,
and that they're both good fliers.

Suddenly, Neal flies straight toward you, cocking his
fist for a punch. You shoot to the left, dodging out of
the way—and Le Chèvre hits you from other side with
a double kick. You spin around and then regain control.
The two operatives circle you again, getting ready for
their next strike. You wonder if you should have given
the jetpack to Carmen instead. At least she has some
fighting experience.

Your only chance is your superior flying skill. Putting
your jetpack to full power, you fly straight up into the
air, one hundred feet, then two hundred feet. Le Chèvre
and Neal the Eel follow. You go higher, higher, higher,
until the two ships look like toy boats in a bathtub down

below. You don't have much fear of heights, but you've never been this high before in a jetpack. You feel tiny and alone.

No time to be afraid. Turning downward, you go into a power dive, using your jetpack to speed toward the water, faster even than falling. Le Chèvre and Neal the Eel dodge out of the way as you pass, and then dive to chase you. Down, down, down—the surface of the water comes closer at terrifying speed.

At the last possible moment, you somersault in the air and fire your jetpack engines full power upward. Your feet dip into the cold ocean as you change direction. On either side of you, Le Chèvre and Neal the Eel try to make the same turn, but they're not as skilled as you, and both plunge into the water.

Carmen, Zack, and Ivy cheer from the deck of the *Narwhal*. Then Carmen points to the VILE ship, which is turning to escape. You fly over and land on the deck. Inside the cabin, you see Dr. Bellum herself working the ship's controls. When she sees you, she looks up in alarm and races out onto the deck.

"Who are you?" she gasps.

"I was an engineer at Zeta Circuits," you say. "But I'm on Carmen's team now."

"Perhaps you should join *my* team," she says. "I am Dr. Saira Bellum, the greatest criminal scientist in the world. We work on the most spectacular projects—death rays, giant robots, mind-control devices."

"I don't think so," you say.

"Wait," she pleads. "Anything that you can imagine we can build. We have limitless resources. And we don't worry about little things like morality or the law."

You pause for just a moment, imagining the things that you could build.

"I can see you are considering my offer," Bellum says, stepping toward you and holding out her hand.

WHAT DO YOU DO?

▷ If you join Bellum, turn to page **56**.

▷ If you drop Bellum in the ocean,
   turn to page **107**.

You fling the metal ball back at Mime Bomb, who catches it, spins around, and tosses it underhand high in the air. As the ball flies, it buzzes louder, sparks of electricity shooting from its surface. Suddenly, you feel a jolt run through your body, and everything goes dark.

When you wake up, you are in the back of a van with no windows, riding on a bumpy road. You are sitting on a bench, your hands tied behind your back and attached to the wall of the van, so you can't stand or move. Carmen, Zack, and Ivy are next to you on the bench, tied up the same way.

Mime Bomb sits at the front, a broad grin on his bright red lips.

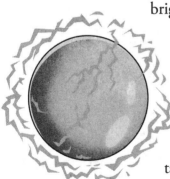

"What happened?" you ask groggily.

"It was a crackle ball," says Carmen. "Dr. Bellum was working on it while I was at school. It shoots bolts of electricity at every target within one hundred feet."

"Then why didn't it hit the mime?"

"His sneakers," Carmen explains. "The thick rubber

soles are insulators against electricity, so the bolts couldn't go through him."

Mime Bomb smiles and lifts his feet to show off the silver sneakers. He pulls a smartphone from his pocket, holding it up for you to see. A woman with round glasses and wild white hair smiles at you from the screen.

"Carmen Sandiego!" the woman says with a smile. "So nice to see you again."

"Dr. Bellum," Carmen replies scornfully. "Where are you taking us?"

"You and your new friends are coming to see me on Vile Island. I assure you, we will have a great deal of fun together."

The screen goes dark. You have a feeling that Vile Island won't be fun at all.

THE END

"YOU SHOULD HAVE the last jetpack," you say, taking it off and handing it to Carmen. "I can teach you how to use it."

"Okay," Carmen says. "Thank you."

Starting the next day, you give Carmen flying lessons, teaching her how to use the control glove to take off and land, control her speed, and turn in the air. She learns quickly, and a few days later, Player calls with information about a new VILE plot that needs to be stopped. You and Carmen say a warm goodbye.

You return to your apartment, where your cat, Mustard, is waiting. You scratch her behind the ears. "Well, Mustard," you say, "looks like my big adventure is over. I'm going to need a new job." There are lots of opportunities for an engineer like you in Singapore, and within a couple of weeks, you get a good job at a company that makes remote-control mini-submarines for kids to play with.

And so, your life goes pretty much back to normal. Late one night, you are playing a strategy game on your computer, when Player's face pops up on the monitor. *"Hey!"* he says. *"Sorry to bother you, but the jetpack is broken. Do you think you could fix it?"*

"Yeah," you say.

"Great," Player says. *"Ivy is right outside your apartment. She'll be up in a minute."*

A moment later, there's a knock on your door. You find Ivy standing in the hall, jetpack in hand. "I fixed it a couple of times," she says. "But this time, I can't figure what's wrong. It seems like the left jet is weak, so Carmen keeps turning right."

"It's probably the air compressor," you say. "They break more than they should. I can replace it, but I don't have the tools I need at home."

Player rents you a workshop in Singapore. For the next couple of days, you and Ivy work together to replace the jetpack's air compressor. Ivy is very good with the mechanical stuff—she says from her days fixing car engines back in Boston. As you're packing up the workshop, Carmen herself shows up at the door.

"I was in the neighborhood," she says, "so I thought I'd drop by."

"The jetpack is fixed, maybe better than ever," Ivy says proudly.

"Great job, thank you," Carmen says. She turns to you. "Maybe you should join our crew permanently. I'd love to see what sort of gadgets you and Ivy could build together. And it's got to be more fun than toy submarines."

Of course, you say that you'll do it. Player arranges for you to keep the workshop, and you and Ivy start brainstorming high-tech gadgets. First, you invent an insect-size drone that Carmen can use to scout ahead on her missions. Then, you create color-changing fabric that lets her camouflage herself like a chameleon. You even build jetpacks for the whole team, so that you, Carmen, Zack, and Ivy can go on flying capers together.

With each passing week, you feel more like part of the crew, proud to be using your skills in the fight against evil.

THE END

Create more exciting adventures
with **CARMEN SANDIEGO**
when you *chase your own caper*

in

ENDGANGERED
OPERATION

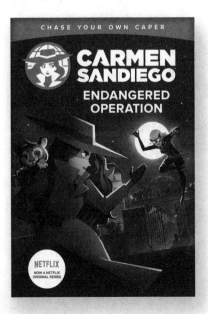
Turn the page for a sneak peak!

VILE PLOT

THE MOOD WAS GRIM in the VILE faculty lounge. The five VILE instructors, leaders of the world's most powerful criminal organization, were meeting to make their plans. Many of VILE's recent schemes had been stopped by their former-student-turned-renegade-thief, Carmen Sandiego. They were looking for ways to make up lost profits.

"I've got a dandy of an opportunity," said Coach Brunt, an enormously strong woman who spoke with a thick Texas drawl. "I am in contact with a very wealthy collector who has offered to pay a fortune for all the items on this list." She slid a piece of paper down the table for the other instructors to see.

Professor Maelstrom picked up the list. He was a stern-looking man with pale skin and a voice that could send shivers up your spine. "Amur tiger, black-footed ferret, hawksbill turtle," he read. "My dear Coach Brunt, is this a list of animals?"

"Not just any animals," Brunt answered with a grin. "Every animal on this list is extremely rare or endangered—which means they're worth a pile of money."

"Disgusting," said Countess Cleo, sticking her nose in the air. As always, she was perfectly dressed in the finest clothes and jewelry. "The only animal I'm interested in is mink."

Dr. Saira Bellum picked up the list. "There are some fascinating creatures here," she said, pushing her glasses up on her nose. "If we decide to move forward, I can arrange for their proper feeding and transportation."

Shadowsan, a master ninja who never smiled, crossed his arms over his chest. "I was not aware that VILE had become a pet store," he growled.

"Lighten up, Shadowsan," said Brunt with a smile. "A great thief can steal anything. Doesn't matter if it's got fur and claws, so long as it makes us a fortune."

"An excellent point," said Maelstrom. "I propose a vote. All in favor of this operation, raise your hands."

Brunt, Maelstrom, and Bellum raised their hands right away. More reluctantly, Cleo and Shadowsan followed. "Outstanding," said Brunt. "Now, which animal shall we capture first?"

Will VILE succeed in their plot to steal the world's rarest animals? In this story, it's up to you. Your choices will lead to one of twenty endings.

ARE YOU READY?

Turn the page.

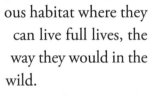

YOU ARE A ZOOKEEPER at the Schönbrunn Zoo in Vienna, Austria.

As you proudly tell visitors, Schönbrunn is the oldest zoo in the world. It was built in 1752 by Emperor Francis Stephen as a place to keep his collection of exotic birds, monkeys, and other creatures. In 1906, it was home to the first baby elephant ever born in a zoo. These days, the zoo keeps more than seven hundred kinds of animals, trying to give them all a generous habitat where they can live full lives, the way they would in the wild.

You love your job, although it's a lot of hard work—feeding the animals, watching for signs of disease or discomfort, cleaning out their living areas. Today, you are looking after the zoo's newest arrival,

Nadezhda, a baby Amur tiger. Amur tigers are the largest type of tiger in the world, living mostly in the birch forests of eastern Russia. They are also an endangered species, with only about five hundred and forty alive in the wild. Nadezhda means "hope" in Russian, because with so few Amur tigers remaining, each one carries the hope of the species.

It's late evening, and the Schönbrunn Zoo is closed to the public for the day. You let yourself into the nursery building where Nadezhda lives. Sadly, her mom wasn't paying enough attention to her, which is not uncommon for first-time tiger moms, so the veterinarians at the zoo decided that she should be fed by hand.

"Nadezhda, suppertime!" you call. She stays in a fenced-in area that takes up almost half the room, full of toys and fun places for a baby tiger to hide. Usually, she toddles out right away when she hears your voice, but today you don't see her. A pang of worry clenches your stomach.

You notice that the back door to the nursery building is open, although it should be closed and locked at this time of night. You look out to see two people fleeing around a row of trees. One of them is a large man holding something about the size of Nadezhda's carrying case.

WHAT DO YOU DO?

▷ Go for help.

▷ Chase the tiger thieves.